Holly Jean

and the Secret of Razorback Ridge

BONNIE COMPTON HANSON

Published by Warner Press Inc, Anderson, IN 46012
Warner Press and "WP" logo is a trademark of Warner Press Inc.

ISBN: 978-1-59317-431-6

Editors: Robin Fogle, Karen Rhodes
Cover by Christian Elden
Photo: Mike Meadows
Design and layout: Curtis D. Corzine
Printed in the USA

Contents

Chapter 1
Black Cows and Blackberries

Cincinnati, Ohio, Late May 1942

"Aaargh!"

With a toss of her copper-red curls, Holly Jean Roberts grabbed her books and slammed her locker shut. "I just hate school!" she grumped. "The teachers act like we're test-taking robots—or Martians!"

Her best friend Shirley Jefferson laughed. "Oh, come on, Jeannie. Tests build character. Isn't that what Principal Prichard's always telling us? Besides, seventh grade's almost over. We've got a whole summer of fun ahead of us. Hey, doofus, where's your flute?"

"Oops." Holly Jean giggled and unlocked her locker. "There we go. Okay, little flute, come to Mama, and let's get out of here."

A few minutes later, the two girls joined the throng of students rushing out of stately Taft Junior High. But even in that crowd, these two stood out—"Jeannie," with her fly-away hair; Shirley, tall and willowy as a ballerina.

"Yea, summer!" Holly Jean bubbled. "If we live so long. At least my birthday's right after school's out. Oh, boy. I'll be thirteen on the thirteenth of June—a real teenager at last!

For my party, Papa Joe and Aunt Bea said I could invite three of my very best friends—including you, of course—to White Castle for burgers and shakes. Then we'll go to a movie down at the Regal—maybe a Judy Garland or Roy Rogers one, or lots of cartoons. Drinks and popcorn too, of course."

By now they had reached busy Walnut Street near their school. "Oh, we won't need to buy any popcorn, motor mouth," teased her friend, as they waited for the light to change. "Not with you always 'popping' off jokes. But, remember, school's not over yet. I've still gotta finish my science project tonight, or else."

"Me, too. Plus practice my flute solo for next week's concert. See our streetcar?"

Shirley glanced at her watch. "Naw, it's not due for another fifteen minutes." Her dark face glowed with good humor. She wore her naturally curly black hair pageboy style, smoothed down and turned under at her neck. But tight little ringlets still managed to dance all around her forehead.

Walnut Street was lined with small shops of every kind— shoe stores, bakeries, hardware stores, food markets—blocks and blocks of them. But the girls' favorite was the Woolworth's 5 & 10, or "dime store," right by their streetcar stop. One of its huge display windows was piled high with laundry detergent, hand lotion, umbrellas, bolts of fabric, swimming suits, and picnic supplies. Plus there were penny loafers with real copper pennies inserted in front.

Holly Jean pointed to the shoes. "Aunt Bea's been saving up my shoe ration stamps for months, so I sure hope I get a new pair of loafers for my birthday. My old ones are practically falling apart, and they're so tight I keep getting blisters. Won't it be great when this war's over, and we can buy all the shoes we want?"

"Why don't you try saddle shoes instead?" Shirley asked. "You have to use two colors of shoe polish on them, but they really look cool and they last a lot longer."

The other window was ablaze with red, white, and blue streamers in honor of the upcoming Memorial Day holiday. Large wreaths of crepe paper flowers and paper flags to put on graves were displayed along with pictures of Armed Services personnel—a soldier, a sailor, a Marine, and smiling young women in crisp WAC, WAVE, and nursing outfits. A scratchy record played *Over There*, while at the top of the window hung a large banner: "World War II—V for Victory."

Holly Jean thought of all the young servicemen fighting overseas in both Europe and the Pacific. War was so awful, especially this one! Pointing at a poster she said, "Look, Shirley. Doesn't that soldier remind you of your brother Jack in his uniform?"

"Not without a bit more suntan," her friend quipped.

Holly Jean blushed. Shirley had been her best friend for two years now—ever since Holly Jean's mother died, and she, Papa Joe, and Aunt Bea moved to this part of town. She often forgot that Shirley's skin was the rich dark brown of walnuts down at Granny Nanny's farm. Well, no matter what her race was, Shirley Jefferson happened to be the nicest, smartest and prettiest girl in the whole school, and Holly Jean was proud to be her friend.

"Oh, I almost forgot!" Holly Jean gasped. "I promised Aunt Bea I'd pick her up a tube of lipstick today. She works such long hours at the defense plant, she hardly ever gets to the store herself."

Rushing inside, the two girls passed aisle after aisle of brooms, hammers, ironing boards, and housedresses. The lipsticks were lined up next to the face powder, hand lotion, and other cosmetics. Giggling, the girls tried on some sample cologne.

While Holly Jean waited at the cash register to pay for the lipstick, she heard, "Hey, Red! Can I treat you girls to a Black Cow?"

She grinned and waved to Roger Bennett, soda-jerking after school over at the lunch counter. A ninth-grader with a blond burr haircut and a big grin, Roger played trumpet in the school orchestra and always called her "Red."

Holly Jean loved his root beer-and-ice cream specials, but today she'd promised her aunt she'd get right home and start dinner. "Sorry, Rog; maybe next time."

Suddenly, they heard it. *Clang! Clang!*

"Come on, Jeannie!" Shirley cried. "There's our streetcar."

They rushed outside just as the big trolley rattled to a stop on its shiny metal tracks. High overhead draped its glistening electric wires, sometimes sparking like Fourth of July fireworks.

After dropping their dimes in the fare box, the girls grabbed a seat. "Doing anything special for Memorial Day?" Shirley asked.

Her friend nodded. "Going to my Granny Nanny's farm in Kentucky to put flowers on Mama Jean's grave. They call it Decoration Day down there, you know. Everyone decorates graves. And you?"

"Picnic at the zoo with my folks. We love that place." Shirley giggled. "We go so often, even the polar bear calls me by my first name! Do you like visiting your grandmother's farm, Jeannie?"

Holly Jean thought of energetic little Granny Nanny and cranky Great-Aunt Kate, living in a narrow valley or "hollow" back in the Cumberland Mountain foothills. "Hickory Hollow," folks around there called it. But Holly Jean liked to call it "Holly Hollow," after the still-flourishing holly tree her great-great-grandfather Ebenezer Roberts had planted there years before. That's how she got her first name. Her middle name was in honor of Mama Jean. Papa Joe said her baby curls reminded them all of brilliant holly berries. In fact, her family still called her "Holly Jean" instead of her more citified nickname of "Jeannie."

Great-Great-Grandfather Ebenezer had also built the tiny log cabin her Granny Nanny and Grandpa Ned moved to when they first got married. Granny Nanny, a widow, still lived there today. Granny's children had all been born there: Uncle Tom, Papa Joe, and Aunt Bea, the youngest. Papa Joe and Aunt Bea moved away when they were grown, but Uncle Tom had a store nearby in the dusty little village of Morgan Mills.

"Well," Holly Jean replied, "on the plus side, there are lots of beautiful trees there. Wildflowers, too. Blackberries and huckleberries are everywhere, and the air's so clean! *But,*" she added, rolling her eyes, "no telephone, no electricity, no bathrooms, no running water, no sidewalks! I mean, no civilization at all! Snakes and lizards are everywhere. And get this, their schoolhouse is just one room; all the kids together, right through the eighth grade. Same with their church building—and no youth group, no Sunday school. And everyone talks with such a horrible drawl!"

Shirley grinned. "Yeah, I know: 'Ya'll come, y'hear?'" When students from south of the Ohio River enrolled at Taft, lots of the kids called them hillbillies and laughed at their accents. Well, Granny Nanny and Aunt Kate talked like that too.

"Plus everyone is so superstitious," Holly Jean added. "Ghosts, magic, stuff like that. They even have feuds. It's awful."

Her friend shuddered. "Well, don't worry about it, kid. You'll never have to live in a place like that. You're going to stay right here in the big city with me forever and ever. We'll even babysit each other's kids when we grow up. Right?"

Holly Jean grinned. "Right. If we ever make it through the seventh grade, of course."

But suddenly Holly Jean felt very strange inside. What if something happened and she had to live in sleepy little Morgan Mills? With her grouchy great-aunt Kate? Nothing could be worse than that! But, of course, God loved her too much to let that happen, right?

But just to make sure: *Oh, please, God,* she prayed, *You'd never make me live in that awful place, would You? Please, PLEASE?*

Chapter 2
"Greetings!"

Suddenly Shirley jumped up. "Whoops—here's our stop!" Grabbing their books, they both yanked on the overhead cord that alerted the driver to stop. Then they scrambled off the streetcar. "See you tomorrow, gal," Shirley called as she headed down her street.

Holly Jean's own street was lined with towering trees, green lawns, and flowering shrubs. Huge old houses had been made over into several apartments each. Because of World War II, thousands of people had poured into Cincinnati to work at its booming defense factories, and there were never enough homes for them all. Indeed, many of her friends lived in tiny metal trailers at crowded trailer parks.

Papa Joe worked the night shift at one of those defense plants—sometimes every day of the week. He was proud of his paychecks and his part in the war effort, but he usually had greasy black streaks across his face and dark circles under his eyes from such long hours. Aunt Bea worked there too, during the day shift. But they all tried to go to church services as a family on Sunday mornings.

At the front door, Holly Jean reached for her family's mail: a note from their landlord, an official-looking envelope from the U.S. Government, and a letter from her grandmother.

She opened the door quietly so as not to awaken her father, still asleep from his long night's work. Putting the mail and her schoolbooks on the hall table, she hurried into the kitchen.

Getting dinner started each evening was her responsibility; Aunt Bea completed the job when she got home. That way they all had a good hot meal together before Papa Joe left for work again.

After peeling a pan full of potatoes, Holly Jean sliced them into a bowl. Next, she emptied a quart of Granny Nanny's homecanned tomatoes into another bowl, and a jar of green beans into a pot, and set the table. Then it was time for homework. Practicing her flute would have to wait till her father woke up.

An hour later, Aunt Bea rushed in after work, her arms filled with fragrant lilac branches. Aunt Bea's hair was styled in a pretty black pompadour, and she had sparkling blue eyes, rosy cheeks, and a laugh like birds singing. "John Perkins picked these for me," she bubbled. "You know, the new guy I work with on the assembly line. Aren't they gorgeous? He thought we could take them to the cemetery in Morgan Mills when we go this weekend. I'll stick them in a jar of water so they won't wilt."

Her face was glowing. But standing there with her greasestained slacks and banged-up lunch pail, she looked as tired and worn-out as Papa Joe.

In a moment Aunt Bea had the potatoes sizzling. Then she turned on the radio for the war news. Papa Joe woke up and listened too. His eyes were the exact same blue as Aunt Bea's, but his hair was the color of Holly Jean's—a little thinner on top, maybe, but every bit as red.

The war news was grim on both the European and Pacific fronts, but when the announcer switched to sports and baseball, Papa Joe brightened. "Hey, those Reds just might win the pennant, after all!" he boomed. A standing joke with her father was that the Cincinnati ball team was named after his and her red hair.

After giving thanks for their food, Aunt Bea served up the fried potatoes. Suddenly Holly Jean remembered: "We got some letters today, folks. One's from Granny Nanny."

"Wonderful," her aunt replied. "Read hers to us while we eat."

Granny Nanny had to leave school after the third grade, so her penciled scrawl was sometimes hard to make out. Holly Jean carefully opened the envelope and read the letter out loud:

Dearest young'uns:

Already feels like summer. Got lots of new radishes, lettuce, and peas. Them climbing roses my Ned planted out front is blooming right hearty too. Now don't pack no vittles to bring us when you come for Decoration Day, 'cause me and Kate got plenty. And Tom keeps us in flour and cornmeal. But, Bea, could you fetch along some white buttons and a black zipper? The one in your Aunt Kate's skirt done tore. Truth to tell, she gained

a wee bit over winter. But don't you tell her I said so.
She could use more of them store-bought spectacles
for reading the Good Book too. Holly Jean, child, sure am
pining to see you. Well, must stop and milk old Star. Have
a good trip here.

    Love,

    Nan Roberts

Suddenly Holly Jean missed Granny Nanny's warm hugs
and merry laughter, and could hardly wait to see her.

"What else came?" Papa Joe asked as he poured ketchup
on his potatoes.

Aunt Bea picked up the other two envelopes. "This one's
from our landlord," she replied, opening it. "Hope he's finally
going to get our bathtub fixed."

Suddenly she paled. "Oh, no, Joe! Mr. Wilson says his
daughter's family is moving here from Lexington. He needs
our apartment for them to live in, starting June first. *Why,
that's Monday—right after the Memorial Day weekend! That's
awful!*"

Then, looking at the other envelope, she turned even
whiter. Shaking, she handed it to Papa Joe. He only had
to read the first line, "Greetings," before he knew the rest.

Setting it down, he announced quietly, "I'm sorry, folks,
but looks like Uncle Sam can't win this war without me. I've
been drafted into the United States Army."

Chapter 3
No Turning Back

The next day at school Holly Jean broke the grim news to everyone.

"Look, guys," she stammered, "I don't know how to tell you this, but I'm moving. This is my very last day here at Taft."

Roger and Shirley both yelled at the very same time. "Jeannie! What happened?"

Glumly, she said, "My whole world's falling apart, that's what. Papa Joe's just been drafted. We have to give up our apartment. Aunt Bea's moving in with some friends."

"Oh, no!" Shirley cried. "What about you?"

Holly Jean could hardly keep from crying. "I have to go live on the farm with Granny Nanny. Oh, but it's not fair—not fair at all!"

Her friends gave her a big hug. "You can stay at my house," Shirley offered. "We always have room for one more."

Roger shook his head. "Shirl, girl, you already have two families living at your place, plus your grandpa. This stupid housing shortage! But surely we can think up something."

But they couldn't.

Her orchestra teacher was just as shocked. "Oh, Jeannie! What on earth will we do for a flute soloist at our concert?"

Her principal just stood there, shaking his head. "But what about your exams? And you say the school you'll be going to is already out for the year? Well, well. This is highly irregular. Highly irregular! I don't even know what to do about all your paperwork."

But in the end he figured something out. Shirley cried and promised to write. So did Roger. But Holly Jean's new address puzzled him. "Just Morgan Mills—that's it? No street address?"

Holly Jean sighed. "Don't worry. My aunt Tillie runs the post office there. She'll make sure I get it." She was too embarrassed to explain that Morgan Mills was so tiny the village post office was just a corner of her uncle Tom's store.

Shirley and Roger helped her clean out her locker. Then she and Shirley had one last root beer float down at Woolworth's with Roger. Handing her his *God Bless America* sheet music, he said, "Think of me when you play it, Red. This war should be over soon; then you can move back here again, and we'll play that song together. It's a deal?" Both he and Shirley gave her their school photos to remember them by.

That night was a blur of packing. Aunt Bea's co-workers helped move her clothes to her new apartment. Papa Joe's and Holly Jean's clothes, pictures, scrapbooks and other precious belongings were crammed into boxes and piled in the car. Her bike was tied with rope onto the back bumper. As to their furniture, dishes, pots and pans, their landlord bought them all for his daughter's family to use.

So just like that, Holly Jean's whole life changed. It was all so final, like the end of their entire family—maybe even her entire life.

When Aunt Bea shook her awake the next morning, it was still dark out. Holly Jean stumbled out of bed, pulled on some clothes, and combed her hair. After breakfast, they all got ready to go. Papa Joe took a picture of their house with his little Brownie camera, while Aunt Bea packed sack lunches. Then, waving good-bye to all their friends, they were on their way.

There was just enough room left in the back seat for Holly Jean to crouch down between all the boxes and bags. She clutched her precious flute case to her heart and tried not to cry.

Up front, her father and aunt tried just as hard to be cheerful. As the miles passed, they told a lot of rollicking tales about growing up in Hickory Hollow. But when Holly Jean glanced up at the rearview mirror, she gulped. Her father's eyes were filled with tears too. Suddenly she realized how wrenching this separation was going to be for all of them.

It's not fair, God! she stormed in her heart. *Why did You let this terrible war happen? And why are You letting this happen to us? Don't You care? I thought You loved us!*

For lunch, she munched on a peanut butter and jelly sandwich and sipped from a jar of warm lemonade. But she could hardly choke anything down. She felt so lost and helpless she closed her eyes so the others would think she was asleep and not talk to her. After a while, she really was.

Many hours and miles later, Holly Jean woke with a start. The car had stopped, but she had no idea where she was. The front seat was empty, but something was reaching in the open back window—something big and dark and noisy and smelly, making horrible sounds.

Headed straight for her face!

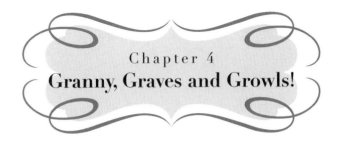

Chapter 4
Granny, Graves and Growls!

Holly Jean screamed at the top of her lungs. "*Help!*"

"Down, Bear!" someone scolded. "You're scaring the poor child to death!"

"Granny Nanny!" Holly Jean rubbed her eyes and looked out.

"Land o' mercy, child!" her grandmother chuckled. "You trying to bust my eardrums? Don't you remember old Bear?"

The huge dog whimpered joyfully, his tail thumping loudly against the fender. Nan Roberts flung open the door and grabbed her granddaughter into her arms.

"Old Bear don't see many children, you know. And I don't see enough myself. Joe said you was so tuckered out you plumb fell asleep. Well, come in, come in! Kate'll sure be tickled to see you!"

Holly Jean kissed her grandmother and stumbled out of the car. The giant brown dog wiggled and whined beside her, begging for a petting. She rubbed his long ears as she looked around. Well, this was it. Hickory Hollow. The very ends of the earth.

Nothing in Hickory Hollow ever seemed to change. Granny's cabin was still weather-beaten and leaning to one side. The richly leafed hills or ridges around her farm remained as steep and high, as forbidding and mysterious as ever. The fields were just as narrow, rocky, and backbreaking to plow.

Bubbling Catfish Creek still tumbled right across the dirt road near the corncrib, but only in flood-time was it deep enough for catfish or much of anything else. The old barn across the meadow still loomed gray and sturdy.

Purple violets and golden dandelions dotted Granny's ragged front yard. Fragrant pink climbing roses and yellow honeysuckle blossoms spilled over the sagging wire fence around her thriving vegetable garden. Chickens scratched in the dust under the huge holly tree that shaded the cabin's porch and stayed green and glowing all year round. That tree was the very one Holly Jean had been named after.

Deep blue irises and fiery tiger lilies surrounded the front porch where Great-Aunt Kate sat in her rocking chair, hugging both Papa Joe and Aunt Bea. Aunt Kate's piercing blue eyes, plump cheeks, and gray-streaked, dark blonde hair were framed by a starched sunbonnet. A crisp white apron covered her long flour-sack dress. Brown cotton stockings, no-nonsense oxfords, and a sturdy cane for her bad knee completed the picture of a virtuous woman farmer.

But not farm *wife*. For "Miss Kate" was an old maid, or spinster. Holly Jean's mother used to call it a real tragedy, but Papa Joe would laugh and say it just proved how smart men were to stay away from her. Knowing how cross and stubborn her great-aunt could be, Jeannie agreed with her father. But

Granny Nanny lived with Aunt Kate, and now Holly Jean had to live with her too!

Granny's sunbonnet was as wide and crisp as her older sister Kate's, her brown hair as salt-and-pepper gray, her skirts as long. She was short and plump, her head barely reaching her granddaughter's shoulder. Everything about her said old and old-fashioned. But under her bonnet brim, her eyes twinkled as brown and merry as Holly Jean's.

Long ago Granny Nanny's husband, Grandpa Ned, had covered the outside of their log cabin with whitewashed boards, though only traces of paint remained now. The chimney was still solid, but moss and small weeds grew on its north side. Aunt Bea swore that poisonous copperheads and rattlesnakes lived deep inside its unmortared stones.

Through the sagging screen door, Holly Jean could see Granny's sitting room. Cozy and small, it featured Aunt Kate's high iron bed, Granny's low wooden one, some cane-bottomed chairs, the fireplace, and a treadle sewing machine. From the lean-to kitchen out back came succulent smells of just-fried chicken, just-baked cake, and ham hock bean soup.

"You sure y'all had lunch?" Granny asked for the umpteenth time.

"Yes, Mama Nan," Aunt Bea replied. "Now we'd better get unpacked and get on to the cemetery before we miss everyone."

She and Holly Jean hauled the boxes and bags to the sagging porch. Papa Joe untied his daughter's blue bike from the back bumper and leaned it up against the corncrib.

"You should get a lot of good exercise, riding it here, Holly Jean," he said. But, looking at the sharp-rocked dirt road, she was sure she'd puncture a tire before she'd gone fifty feet!

Nan Roberts handed a large pair of shears to her son. "Now, Joe, boy, if you'll just clip us some roses and lilies, we can put them in this here bucket. Then we better get on down to the cemetery afore folks think us Robertses don't care none about our dead. We can visit more when we come back. Besides, Tom and Tillie are anxious to see y'all too."

Then they all piled into the car. "Stay!" Granny ordered Bear. And back down the road they bounced to the little Morgan Mills church about a mile away.

Built right next door to a one-room schoolhouse, the ancient, whitewashed church had wide-open doors and a large bell on top. It was surrounded with Model Ts, pickup trucks, horses, mules, and wagons. People in their best Sunday-go-to-meeting dresses and overalls sat in the trucks and wagons and talked. They sat on the wide stone steps and talked. They walked through the cemetery, decorating graves, and talked some more.

For May 30, Memorial or Decoration Day was the biggest holiday of the whole year around here. People came from as far away as Detroit every year to visit with their kinfolk and honor their dead.

The Roberts family made their way slowly across the churchyard, looking for their own relatives' graves. Finding her husband's tombstone, Granny Nanny knelt down and stroked it.

"My Ned, he worked so hard," she said gently. "But he did

love his roses. Look, Ned, sweet, see how thrifty your pink ramblers done turned out?" And she covered his grave with fragrant blossoms.

Aunt Bea and Papa Joe stood teary-eyed beside her. Then they decorated several other graves belonging to family members.

As they walked through the cemetery, they came to a tall, ornate tombstone almost covered by weeds and briars that read, "Maybelle Morgan."

Aunt Kate dabbed at her eyes. "Now ain't that a crying shame!" she exclaimed. "No one's cared for that grave in years, poor woman!" She yanked up the weeds by hand; then placed a bouquet of daisies by the stone.

Last of all, they came to a tombstone so new its white granite shimmered in the brilliant sunshine. A holly leaf was carved on it, with the words: "Jean Jefferson Roberts. She walked in love. Now she walks with angels."

Holly Jean froze. Two years ago, she had a delightful mother who loved her very much. Mama Jean had hair as rich and brown as the earth itself. She was always helping people, and she loved to tell jokes, even when she forgot the punch lines. Then a terrible car accident, and just like that her mother was gone.

Now Papa Joe and Aunt Bea were deserting her as well. Maybe Papa Joe would get shot down in this terrible war, and she'd never see him again and….

Sobbing, she spread Aunt Bea's lilacs, her mother's favorite, across the grave. "Oh, Mama Jean," she whispered, "why did you leave us? Why aren't you here to help me now?"

Beside her, Papa Joe held her tightly. "Don't worry, little girl," he choked. "I'm only going away for a little while to help our nation fight for freedom. Then I'll be back, I promise."

A few minutes later, they walked across the dusty road from the churchyard to the general store run by Papa Joe's older brother, Uncle Tom. Even though this was a holiday, the store was open, for today was its busiest day of the entire year.

The motor on the soda pop cooler rumbled overtime, trying to keep up with all the bottles going in and out. The pickle jars, baloney, and boxes of crackers disappeared as fast as Uncle Tom brought them out. Aunt Tillie cheerfully sold stamps and dispensed free gossip at the postal window. Outside, the tall, glasstopped gasoline pump gurgled and clanged. Indeed, the only quiet spot around was the front store window where Whitey the cat napped, oblivious to all the dust and commotion.

A large man, with black hair like his younger sister Bea, Uncle Tom always wore a white starched shirt, black pants, gray leather vest, cowboy boots, and a big silver belt buckle.

Aunt Tillie was as slim as her husband was heavy. She pulled her thin, sandy hair up into a stern topknot. As possessor of the biggest heart and most sympathetic ears in all of Morgan Mills, she was always busy about other people's problems, whether they wanted her to be or not!

"Well, Holly Jean, gal, you done growed up pretty as a holly berry!" her uncle greeted her. "Come on in, girl. What do you want? Orange pop? Root beer? Potato chips? Hey, think your pa's got enough meat on his bones to be a soldier like my boy Willie?" He laughed heartily, pointing to his own generous waist in contrast to his younger brother's trim one.

Holly Jean thought of her cousin, good-natured Willie. In the middle of his senior year at high school, he had enlisted the day after the Japanese attacked Pearl Harbor, shipping right out to the Pacific. No one had heard from him for weeks now. *Willie, please get this stupid war over and come home safe and sound.*

Suddenly, the thunder of hooves! Yelling and screams!

"What the Sam Hill?" exploded Uncle Tom. Then he and the other men ran outside, while the womenfolk and children crouched behind the old store counter for protection.

"Oh, no!" Aunt Kate moaned. "Ten to one it's Madman Max—*again!*"

Trembling, she sank to the floor. "Lord, Lord, which of us poor souls is he after now? Ain't this trouble ever going to stop?"

With a howl of alarm, Uncle Tom's startled cat leaped from the store window right into Holly Jean's arms. She glanced out the window just as a ferocious-looking man on horseback looked in. Straight at *her.*

He had a white, grizzled beard and a filthy straw hat. One hand waved a huge horsewhip as he squinted through the store window's dusty glass. Suddenly his mouth dropped open. Howling, he whirled around and galloped off down the road.

Soon Uncle Tom and the other men came back inside. Her uncle shook his head. "That fool Morgan!" he exploded. "Ain't no sense whatsoever in that man's head! I swear he's possessed!"

Aunt Kate pounded her cane on the floor. "Menace to humanity, he is! God as my witness, I wish the sheriff would haul that skunk off afore he hurts someone else. Already kilt four men, I hear, not counting his own poor Maybelle."

Aunt Tillie shivered. "Only four? I heared tell it was five!"

Papa Joe put his arm around his still shaking daughter. "Now ladies, those are just rumors and you know it." To Holly Jean, he said, "Honey, just forget what you saw. Max Morgan's long gone by now."

Uncle Tom nodded. "Yep. Way he was riding he's probably all the way back up Razorback Ridge by this time. Good riddance too."

Holly Jean cuddled the still-trembling cat. "Razorback Ridge? Is that anywhere around here, Uncle Tom?"

He laughed out loud. "Land o' Goshen, child, don't you know? It's the big hill back of your own Granny's house—right smack where you're gonna be living."

"Don't you never go up that hill, girl," Aunt Kate warned. "It's haunted!"

Granny scowled. "Mind your mouth, Kate Barkley!" she snapped. "No need to scare the poor child more than she is already."

Her sister folded her ample arms and scowled right back. "Now don't you try belittling me, Nan Roberts. I-I never told a soul, but I seed a vision up there just this last week, I did—right afore Joe, Bea, and Holly Jean come. A vision of things from another world, a vision of whiteness, a vision of *death*."

She pointed her cane at Holly Jean. "That hill is accursed, young lady, and all of them what lives on it. Stay off, or face the wrath of God!"

Papa Joe put his arm around Kate's ample waist. "Now, Aunt Kate, I walked all over that hill near' every day, all my growing-up years. I reckon if there were ghosts up there, I'd seen at least one of them. That kind of talk's not God-honoring, anyway." More brightly, he said, "Say, how about us all heading back up the hollow and having some of Ma's good fried chicken? And Aunt Kate's famous lemon pie!"

Back at the farm, they gathered around the old kitchen table, its red-checked oilcloth piled high with chicken, pickled cabbage, string beans, mashed potatoes, and cornbread. As Papa Joe led in saying grace, Holly Jean tried to remember his words, to think about after he was gone.

After dinner, Aunt Bea and Holly Jean washed the dishes in a big metal dishpan, while Papa Joe and Granny went to the pasture after Star. He milked the gentle Jersey cow; then lowered the bucket of fresh milk down into the well to cool.

With the hill behind them now deep in shadow, they all moved out to the front porch to enjoy the evening breeze. Bear plopped his head down on Holly Jean's lap and gazed at her adoringly. Granny worked her butter churn, while Aunt Bea sewed a new zipper into Aunt Kate's skirt.

As for Aunt Kate herself, she peered about in her brand-new reading glasses and declared, "Nan, did you see what them trashy Wilson folk did today? Put cheap paper flowers on their kins' graves, they did, 'stead of proper real ones. And the skirts on that hussy, Belle Higgs! Hiked above her knees till I was 'shamed to look! Not to mention that Johnson girl wearing pants like a man. Don't know what this world is a-coming to!"

"Now, Aunt Kate!" Aunt Bea retorted. "Women are supposed to wear short skirts these days to save fabric for the war effort. As for slacks, I wear them to work myself. They're far more modest in a defense factory than skirts."

Her aunt harrumphed and reached for her corncob pipe. "Well, I still calls it shameful. Just like that Max Morgan.

An insult to all us law-abidin' folk. He should be rode out of the county on a rail!"

Granny frowned. "Kate, the good Lord's to judge, not us. You know good and well Mr. Max was always a hard worker. Ain't never heared of him doing nothin' dishonest, and he was a good neighbor to my Ned 'way back when."

Papa Joe nodded. "I remember him helping us get the hay and corn in the year Pa broke his leg. His daughter Daisy was in my class at school—such a shy little thing. Mr. Max used to bring her down the mountain every morning on his mule, rain or shine. A fair man and a good father he was. Leastways, till his troubles started."

Holly Jean leaned against Granny's rocking chair. "What troubles, Papa Joe?"

Aunt Kate pounded the porch floor with her cane. "God's revenge that's what! One day his wife was healthy as an ox, and next day poor Maybelle was nailed up in a coffin— her blood-red hair in a dark, cold grave, and her blood on someone's hands. Max carrying on like a mad man, and that girl of their'n never being seed again. *I* say he done did away with them both, that's what *I* say! Yes, their poor souls haunts Razorback Ridge to this very day. For them as died violent can never rest in peace."

"Shh! Enough of this talk, Kate!" Granny scolded. "We'uns won't be together again for a long spell. Bea's got to go back to the city to work, and who knows where my Joe has to go. So let's enjoy each other while we can." More cheerfully, she added, "How about some strawberries with Star's good cream, Joe? Bea, you and Holly Jean can serve us up some, and put the coffeepot back on, if you will. Aunt Kate is partial to a good strong cup afore bedtime. Maybe Joe would like one too."

Kate pulled her shawl closer around her plump shoulders. "Guess I'll pass on the berries. But how about bringing me a piece of my fresh lemon pie? Best lemon pie in three counties, John Higgs used to say. Fellows fought over my pies every pie social ever I went to. It's the meringue, you know; got to get it just right. Joe, can I talk you into a piece, boy?"

He grinned and gave her a peck on the cheek. "I just might have the berries and pie both, Aunt Kate! The coffee too. It'll be a long time before I have good home cooking like this again."

In the kitchen, Holly Jean grumbled, "Aunt Bea, how in the world can I stand living with a grouchy old pill like Aunt Kate? I think I'll just die!"

Her aunt laughed, her twinkling eyes as blue as huckleberries. "Oh, she's not so bad, kid. Be like Granny. Show her love, but don't let her put anything over on you."

"Did you know Madman Max when you lived here?"

"Well, yes and no. I was kind of young when his wife died, and I didn't know Crazy Daisy very well."

"Crazy Daisy?"

Aunt Bea smiled wryly. "His little daughter, Daisy. Of course, it wasn't kind of them, but folks around here used to call her that. She was so sweet and different. Talked to trees and animals—stuff like that. She had long blonde hair and was very pretty, but too shy for anyone to get to know her."

"Land sakes, Bea!" Aunt Kate called from the porch. "Them skeeters will be biting soon. Where's our pie?"

After dessert, everyone's mood was much sweeter. Granny and Aunt Kate entertained them with merry tales from the past. Then the fireflies came out, and Holly Jean raced around with Bear, catching some in a canning jar.

When at last it was time to go back inside, Granny lit the kerosene lamp, and they all talked some more.

Finally, Granny said, "Well, children, them chickens went to roost a long time ago. Tomorrow's the Lord's day and church, so we better get some shut-eye too."

Because the cabin was so tiny, Granny had prepared some "guest rooms" elsewhere. She had piled one homemade feather mattress on top of the corn in the corncrib for Papa Joe to sleep on. Then she carried another one up the wobbly outside ladder to the attic for Holly Jean and Aunt Bea. With plenty of pillows and quilts, everyone was made comfortable for the night.

As Holly Jean and her aunt hurried outside with a flashlight and the jar of fireflies, they found the ladder full of roosting chickens. Aunt Bea shooed them off and started up to the small attic door, with her niece close behind her. Bear whined below, unable to follow, then headed out to the corncrib to find Papa Joe.

As they climbed the rickety rungs, a full moon rose over Briar Hill on the other side of the hollow. Whip-poor-wills called through the warm, friendly dark. Crickets and tree frogs chirped.

The door to the attic was just high enough to crawl through. Inside, the ceiling was so low they could barely sit up. Holly Jean and her aunt undressed in the dark and slipped under the covers. The jar of fireflies twinkled beside them as the golden moon peeked in through the small attic door. It was almost like camping out!

"Aunt Bea," Holly Jean finally whispered. "Do you think Mr. Morgan really killed his wife and daughter?"

"Don't listen to such gossip, dear. They probably died of the flu or typhoid fever, or maybe in an accident of some sort. When people live so far away from doctors, it's hard to get help in time, you know."

"Oh." Holly Jean was quiet again for a while. Then she said, "Aunt Bea, I'm going to miss you so much! I hope you like being with your girlfriends, but I sure wish we didn't have to give up our own place. You were so much fun to live with. Will you come visit me as soon as you can? And this John you work with—are you going to marry him? And can I be in your wedding?"

Her aunt giggled. "Silly girl. Of course, I'll come visit as soon as I can. As to John, how should I know whether I'll marry him or not? We've barely met. But I do like him a lot. We're going to go to church together next Sunday if we both are off work."

Suddenly Aunt Kate pounded her cane on the ceiling beneath them. "Quiet, up there! Confound it! Can't a body get some decent sleep?"

Holding tightly to her aunt's hand, Holly Jean drifted off to sleep herself, dreaming troubled dreams of sad, sweet ghosts with shimmering hair.

And new green graves in the churchyard.

The next morning, after feasting on sausage, scrambled eggs, wild strawberries, and Granny's hot biscuits, Papa Joe drove them back to Morgan Mills for Sunday morning worship service. Long before they reached the village, they could hear welcoming church bells, echoing sweetly from mountain to mountain.

Although the cemetery was still bright with yesterday's bouquets, the crowd had quite disappeared. Today only one Model T Ford and two mules waited outside. Papa Joe always said Morgan Mills' folks loved their church, but they'd just as soon wait until they were planted in the churchyard to have to be there every single Sunday!

Inside, the one-room building was plain but clean. Stiff wooden benches filled the room, with a potbellied stove in the middle. A bedraggled piano stood in one corner, a stack of firewood in another. Up front on a small platform sat the pastor, "Brother Jake" Morgan, Madman Max's brother.

Holly Jean thought of the large, lively church she attended in the city, with stained glass windows, padded pews, and pealing organ. With a Sunday school full of laughing boys and girls, as well as grown-ups of all ages. Where Papa Joe sang in the choir, and Aunt Bea helped out in the nursery on the Sundays she didn't have to work.

She also remembered her best friend Shirley's smaller church, with its joyful choir, hands clapping, _Amens_ and _Hallelujahs_. Dear Shirley, the prettiest and smartest girl in all of Taft Junior High, with skin like dark, rich wood and laughter as merry as bells ringing. Holly Jean missed her already.

And then there was _this_ church! Aunt Tillie sat on the front row in her best bonnet. Scattered around her were three older women, two older men, one girl Holly Jean's age, one young woman with two babies, and one without any. That was it. The entire congregation!

Except, of course, for Holly Jean's own family. She sat proudly between her father and pretty, young aunt. How she was going to miss them both!

Finally, Brother Jake stood up to lead the singing. Since he had the only hymnbook, people had to follow along as best they could. No one even tried to play the banged-up piano. Fortunately, Papa Joe knew all the songs and boomed them out as loud as a whole choir. So did Aunt Kate.

Then the pastor began preaching about having good character (which he pronounced "kee-rick-ter") and needing to do right and live by the Bible. The sermon seemed to last forever. Bored, Holly Jean began leafing through the Bible her mother gave her for her eighth birthday. Turning to Psalm 56:3, she read: "What time I am afraid, I will trust in Thee."

Dear God, she prayed quietly, *please help me not be afraid for Aunt Bea and Papa Joe to leave me here. Help me be a good helper to Granny Nanny and Aunt Kate and not to mind so much being stuck out here away from everything else in the world.*

She wanted to add, "And from every*one* else too, like my best friend Shirley, and Roger, and all the other kids from school I was going to invite to my birthday party next week." But she wasn't sure God would think that was important, compared with the terrible war and everything else He had to take care of. So instead, she prayed, *Please take care of Papa Joe and Cousin Willie in the war. And tell Mama Jean up there with You that I love her.*

After the service, the pretty young woman without a baby said, "Why, you must be Miss Holly Jean Roberts! I'm Linda Wilson, the teacher here at Morgan Mills Elementary School."

Miss Wilson had soft brown hair and twinkly gray eyes. "Welcome to Morgan Mills, my dear. You've probably already seen our school—that red, one-room building just the other side of the cemetery. Classes for this year were over last week, but they'll start up again in August. I look forward to having you join us."

Having to go back to *grade* school? What a letdown! But Holly Jean tried to be polite. "Glad to meet you, Miss Wilson. But everyone at my old school called me 'Jeannie.'"

The teacher laughed. "And everyone at school here calls me 'Miss Linda,' so you're welcome to as well." Then turning to the young girl Holly Jean had noticed, she said, "This is Tootsie Anderson, Jeannie. Tootsie, this is Miz Nanny's granddaughter. Won't it be nice to have another girl your age in our school?"

Tootsie had frizzled blonde hair and a smirk. "Why, Miss Jeannie!" she giggled. "Such a pleasure to see y'all. Imagine! Getting to meet a genuine city slicker with a Yankee accent as shrill as a wet cat's! Ooo, a pleasure indeed!" And she waltzed right out the front door.

Miss Linda blushed. "Oh, I'm sorry, dear. Tootsie does have a bit of a tongue." She laughed. "All right, she has *lots* of tongue! But I'm really glad your folks brought you today. My own family goes to a big church in Willow Bend where I live, but I come here when I can to encourage Brother Jake and the children of this community. Hope to see you again next Sunday."

After meeting Tootsie Anderson, Holly Jean wasn't sure she ever wanted to go there again! *Dear God*, she prayed sadly, *why did You stick me out here in Never-Never Land? Don't You love me anymore?*

Back at Granny's, Papa Joe invited his daughter and Bear to join him as he roamed around the farm before dinner.

"I figure it'll be a long while before I'm back here again, Holly Jean," he said. "I want to memorize everything about it for when I'm gone. But before we go, be sure and change to your jeans and high-top gym shoes. Low school shoes aren't much good on a mountain farm like this. You always need your feet and ankles covered up against ticks, chiggers, and snakes."

In the old barn, piles of weathered tobacco sticks sprawled in one corner under an empty hayloft, along with several bales of hay. Cackling chickens and ducks seemed to be everywhere.

Morgie, the mule, nuzzled Papa Joe for a petting. "Your Grandpa Ned bought him from Max Morgan's father," Papa Joe said. "That's why your Grandpa named him 'Morgie.' Hershell Morgan raised the best mules in the whole county." Old Morgie was now retired, except for pulling Granny's plow once or twice a year or hauling corn to the mill to be ground.

They sat down on the hay to look around. Holly Jean loved its dry sweetness that still smelled of last summer's clover.

Suddenly she heard a squeak. Something small and furry scurried by her feet.

Bear barked. "Mice?" she cried.

Papa Joe laughed. "No. Kittens. Wait, maybe they'll come out again for us. Here, hold Bear still a minute."

Sure enough, in a moment four little bundles of fur scampered in front of her, rolling and playing with each other. But when she reached out her hand to pet them, they scrambled away, mewing plaintively.

"Barn cats," her father explained. "They're wild."

Then they hiked across the pasture. "Looks like the blackberries are already getting ripe," Papa Joe said. "Huckleberries will be soon too. Your grandmother will want you to help her pick a lot of them to make pies and jam and jelly. And you know what good pies and jam and jelly she and Aunt Kate make!"

Next, they climbed Briar Hill, through open meadows and dense hardwood forests. Coming back down farther west, they crossed Catfish Creek and headed up the other side—the hill behind Granny Nanny's cabin.

Holly Jean giggled. "Oooo, this is scary. Aren't we going up that spooky Razorback Ridge now?" But she didn't feel half as brave as she sounded.

"Never you mind Aunt Kate and her tall tales," her father replied. "There's a special place up here I want you to see. I used to come here all the time when I was a boy."

After hiking a mile or so around rugged boulders and

through thick piles of leaves, they suddenly came to a deep ravine. Its banks were carpeted with maidenhair ferns, mayflowers, and Indian paintbrushes. A tiny, babbling stream rushed down the middle—suddenly plunging over a breathtaking series of waterfalls.

"The best time to see these falls is in the spring," Papa Joe explained. "By the end of summer they always dry up."

Holly Jean was awestruck. "What are they called?"

"The falls? Well, don't reckon anyone ever gave them a name."

"Then I will." Picking up a fallen branch, she held it over the ravine and proclaimed grandly, "I now dub thee the Haunted Waterfall."

Her father threw back his head and laughed. "Well, that's as good a name as any, I reckon. Holly Jean, this is a great place to sit and think when you've got problems."

She thought of Aunt Kate and that snooty Tootsie Anderson. Of Papa Joe going off to war, and missing him, Aunt Bea, Shirley, Roger, and her teachers and all her friends at church and school. Yes, she would probably have plenty of problems to sit and think about in the days ahead!

Back at the house, dinner was ready. Afterwards, her father and Aunt Bea headed out to the car. Aunt Bea opened the trunk and pulled out a large package, wrapped in glittering paper with a silvery bow. "Happy birthday, Holly Jean. Hope you like this, but don't open it till the big day!"

So her aunt did remember her birthday, after all! The package was about the size of a shoebox—maybe those new shoes she was hoping for. Just in time too. She had only two pair of shoes left—her school shoes and gym shoes, and both pairs were falling apart.

Next, Papa Joe reached into his pocket and brought out a shiny coin. "Dear, your Grandpa Ned gave me this 'lucky' silver dollar when I left home for work in the big city. I'd like for you to have it now, to keep always."

He placed it gently in Holly Jean's right hand. Then he put a crisp five-dollar bill in her left one.

"The five bucks is yours to spend," he explained. "You might need some clothes or something before I have a chance to send you more."

Holly Jean hugged her father and aunt, her eyes stinging with tears. "Oh, I'm going to miss you both so much!" she sobbed.

After a big round of farewells, Granny handed Aunt Bea a box of leftover chicken and cornbread to eat on the long trip home.

"Well, well, too much excitement around here for these old bones," Aunt Kate grumbled. "Think I'll get myself inside and take a nap."

Granny Nanny wiped her eyes. "Guess I might as well make a little apple cobbler for the week," she replied. "Them apples in the root cellar are starting to go bad these warm days."

Holly Jean looked at them both. As much as she loved Granny Nanny, she had never felt so alone. "Maybe I'll just take a walk," she said to no one in particular.

Up in the attic, she put Aunt Bea's present away to open on her birthday the following Saturday. Then, taking her flute, she headed back up to the falls Papa Joe had shown her, an eager Bear romping along beside her.

Once there, she found a comfortable spot on the soft moss, Bear's head on her lap. Then slowly and sadly she played *God Bless America*—the solo she would have been performing this week at her school's Spring Concert back in Cincinnati—the song she would have played with Roger. Hundreds of people would have heard her there. What fun to have them applaud her! Especially Papa Joe and Aunt Bea. And Shirley. With Roger over in the trumpet section whispering, as he always did, "Right on, Red. Way to go!"

Now there was no one to hear her except a few noisy birds and a sleepy, flea-bitten dog.

Holly Jean played the song over and over, each time feeling more and more miserable.

Suddenly Bear growled—the hair straight up on the back of his neck. There, just beyond an old oak tree was something so white it glittered with an unearthly glow.

The Ghost of Razorback Ridge?

Chapter 8
Chickens and Checkers

Holly Jean leapt up so quickly she almost tumbled over the falls. "H-Hello, there!" she called.

With a roar, Bear charged after their "ghost," but it had vanished. Completely.

Whining in disbelief, the dog dashed around in circles, sniffing frantically. Finally, he returned, dejected. Still shivering herself, she gave him a hug. Then, picking up her flute, she ran full-tilt down the hill. Had she really seen a ghost, or something else? If so, what? And was it good or bad? Or had she just imagined the whole thing?

That week Holly Jean was almost too busy to be lonely. There were so many chores to do, so much to learn. Pick peas, plant potatoes, feed chickens, gather eggs, "slop" hogs. Lead Old Morgie and Star to pasture. Bring them back.

Next, carry loads of wood from the woodpile to the kitchen stove. Haul buckets of wash water from the well. Heat them on the stove. Rub clothes on a washboard. Hang them up outside to dry. Dip them in starch. Sprinkle and roll them up into damp balls. Then use heavy, nonelectric irons heated on the stove. The work never seemed to get done!

Because of her bad knee, Aunt Kate did mostly sitting tasks, such as cooking and ironing. Granny and Holly Jean did all the walking and carrying ones. Soon Holly Jean began to suspect that Aunt Kate didn't have a *bad* knee, after all— just a *good* excuse!

Every day she felt more and more sad. She worried about what she saw up at the falls and didn't know whether to say anything to Granny about it. She also dreaded having Friday come—the day of the big Spring Concert back at her old school. The concert she wouldn't be playing in. And she missed Aunt Bea and Papa Joe and all her old friends and teachers so much! As for her party-less birthday on Saturday.... Well, by Friday she could hardly even smile anymore.

Granny noticed. "Holly Jean, dear, how 'bout heading on down to Tom's store and picking up a few things for me 'n Kate? It'll do you good to get away from us old biddies for a while."

Holly Jean wrote down Granny's list: flour, baking powder, sugar, black shoe polish. "Oh, and some horse liniment too," her grandmother added. "Old Morgie's getting a little down in his back these days."

"And some liver pills for me," Aunt Kate added. "I get down in my back too, you know."

Since arriving at Granny's, Holly Jean had mostly either worn her old gym shoes or gone barefoot. Today, wanting to feel more dressed up for a change, she put on her old school loafers.

Skipping down the hot, dusty road, she giggled to herself, imagining old Morgie the mule and Aunt Kate stretched out together in bed, getting their backs and knees rubbed with horse liniment!

Little Catfish Creek rambled back and forth across Granny's narrow valley. Each time it crossed the bridgeless dirt road, she either jumped over it, stone to stone, or walked around it on the grassy bank. The fields were full of daisies, Queen Anne's lace, and black-eyed Susans. Overhead, the sky was bright and warm. Bobwhites called, and grasshoppers flew up before her. In spite of herself, by the time she reached Morgan Mills, she felt good about the world.

At the store, Aunt Tillie sang out, "Howdy, there, Miss Holly Jean! You won't believe all the mail that done come in for you this week." She handed over a picture postcard and two large envelopes, plus a letter for Granny and a *Grit* magazine for Aunt Kate.

Holly Jean decided not to look at her own mail till her birthday the next day—the one that would make her a teenager at last. The birthday she once thought would be the best in her entire life, but would now probably be the worst!

After Uncle Tom filled Granny's order, he came out from behind the counter, grinning from ear to ear, his hands behind his ample back. "Well, well, young lady!" he exclaimed. "Think it's your birthday or something?" And he held out a brand-new set of checkers. "Ever played?" he asked.

She shook her head. "I've played Chinese Checkers."

"Ha! Forget that fureigner stuff. This is the real, genuine, star-spangled, teetotally American kind! I'm going to keep your birthday set right here next to the cash register. And next time you come, I'll show you how to play like a true champion."

"What he means," retorted Aunt Tillie, "is he'll show you how to waste time like a true champion." Then she winked. "Yes, happy birthday, dear. Tell Granny and Aunt Kate howdy for us. And let Kate know I'm sorry about her bad back. Tell her I said sometimes a cup of nice sassafras tea helps. Or even throwing a pinch of salt over her shoulder when the moon's right."

Skipping along the rocky road back to Granny's, Holly Jean giggled. She pictured Aunt Kate trying to toss salt over her plump shoulders—*really* throwing her back out! Then halfway up the hollow, she suddenly found herself skipping in bare feet. Her school shoes had fallen completely apart!

Bear sniffed disapprovingly at their remains. "That's okay, Bear," Holly Jean laughed. "I'm sure Aunt Bea got me some new ones for my birthday. Anyway, being barefoot's kind of fun!"

The next morning after breakfast, Granny asked, "Holly Jean, dear, how would you like to go fishing today?"

"You mean there's actually fish around here big enough to catch and eat?"

Granny grinned. "Yessirree! Of course now, our own little Catfish Creek only got minnows. But down at the end of the hollow, where Catfish empties into East Fork of Big Willow, they's a right-sized pond. Max Morgan's old man Hershell had his mills there years back, afore they burnt down. That's what Morgan Mills is named for, you know. Well, wait'll you see the catfish there—big as a frying pan! Sometimes trout too—so eager to be caught they practically jump into your arms."

Holly Jean laughed. "But I don't want to catch them in my arms, and we don't have any poles."

Aunt Kate chuckled. "Land sakes, 'course we do! Nanny 'n me fish all the time, child. Only thing I'm better at than baking lemon pies is catching a mess of fish."

Holly Jean was shocked. "You mean *you'd* go with us, Aunt Kate? With your bad knee and all?"

"Try and stop me. Don't have to stand up to fish."

Granny Nanny took off her apron. "Then it's settled. We're all gonna skedaddle down the road for a little birthday fishing party. See, Holly Jean, you thought us old biddies done forgot your birthday, didn't you? Well, no way. Wait'll you see what we'uns been a-planning for you!"

And she gave her granddaughter a big wink.

Her grandmother held up a bucket full of pink, wiggly worms. "See, child, I've already dug up our bait. Ain't they lively? And lunch is in that there picnic bucket. Just don't get the two buckets mixed up! Kate, you can fetch us a quilt for settin' on. Oh, and Holly Jean, could you keep that fool dog out from underfoot till we're ready?"

Holly Jean slipped on her old gym shoes, gathered up her unopened birthday cards and the present Aunt Bea had given her, and they all set off.

Half an hour later, their narrow hollow opened up into a broad, rolling valley. There, by the overgrown ruins of the mills, little Catfish Creek merged with the larger stream, producing a deep, quiet pool. A gentle breeze silvered the leaves of a sheltering sycamore and sent ripples across the crystal-clear water.

"Now you're going to see some good fishing, Holly Jean, girl," Aunt Kate declared. "But first we gotta bait our hooks."

Holly Jean thought she would throw up doing it, but she finally got her worm hooked and her line in the water. Aunt

Kate spread out the quilt and threw her own line in. Then, pulling her sunbonnet down over her face, she promptly went to sleep.

Granny Nanny winked. "Listen to that old gal snore. It'll scare the fish away for sure."

But not only did it not scare the fish away, Aunt Kate, even asleep, caught more than the other two combined.

After a while, Granny unpacked peanut butter sandwiches, some potato salad, pickles, and a tiny birthday cake no bigger than a cookie, covered with pink peppermint icing.

"Baked it in my biscuit cutter, I did," she chuckled. "Now, Kate, let's you and me sing 'Happy Birthday' to this-here grown-up gal."

After gobbling up her tiny cake, Holly Jean looked at her birthday mail. The postcard had a sad little dog on one side. The other side said: "Happy birthday, Red. I sure miss you. Hope to see you soon. Your old trumpet-tooter, Roger."

She thought of Roger's wide, crooked grin, his long, gangly arms, his jokes, and the sweet notes he pulled from his trumpet. *See me soon, Roger? We'll probably never get to see each other again as long as we live!*

Aunt Bea's birthday card pictured a laughing girl in plaid skirt, bobby sox, and saddle shoes. "Happy birthday, keen teen!" it said. "Now the fun begins."

Holly Jean sighed. Ha! Fishing, ironing, and feeding chickens? A lot of fun that was!

The other envelope was from Shirley. "Miss you, kid," she wrote. "They had to cancel the flute solo, 'cause no one else could do it as good as you. Some of us kids got together and took a picture for you so you don't forget us. Happy birthday!"

She shared the snapshot of her friends. Aunt Kate frowned. "Why, Holly Jean! One of these seems to be a black girl. You don't mean she went to school with you, do you?"

Holly Jean stiffened. "Shirley Jefferson is my very best friend, Aunt Kate," she replied. "Of course, we went to school together."

Her great-aunt rolled her eyes. "Well, we ain't got none of her type in these here parts, and, if you don't mind my saying so, that's just the way we like it."

Holly Jean was so angry she jumped right up. "For shame, Aunt Kate! I *do* mind you talking like that! That's a horrible thing to say! God made Shirley just like He made me and you, and God loves her just as much, so there."

"Here, here," Granny Nanny interrupted. "That ain't the way to have us a party. Holly Jean, dear, I'm proud for you to have friends. They can visit here any time, and welcome. Now let's see what's in your pretty birthday box."

Holly Jean carefully undid the gold paper and silver ribbon of Aunt Bea's present. Just as she had suspected, out fell a pair of shoes, but not everyday school ones. These were fancy dress-up sandals with heels a whole inch high. Aunt Bea must have bought them for her concert—the concert she would never play in now.

"Land sakes!" her grandmother exclaimed. "Grown-up shoes for a grown-up young lady!"

Looking at them and savoring the wonderful smell of new leather, Holly Jean realized something sad. Aunt

Bea had bought these before everything changed. Now she couldn't return them, and she had no more shoe stamps to buy another pair.

But there was more in the box: delicate, rose-decorated stationery with its own matching fountain pen, and a book of hymns for the flute.

Holly Jean glanced quickly through the songbook. "Do you think you could help me learn these hymns, Granny?" she asked.

"It'll be our pleasure, won't it, Kate? Why, here's *The Old Rugged Cross, Amazing Grace,* and *In the Garden.* We sing them all the time at meetin's."

Then Aunt Kate handed her a tiny box. "Holly Jean, child, this is a fancy my own pa made for me when I was your age. I used to call it my 'fairy stone.' Old lady like me got no use wearing such pretties now, so I'd like you to have it."

Aunt Kate's smile was as real as her anger had been just a few minutes before. Would Holly Jean ever figure out this woman?

Opening the box, she lifted out a stone unlike any she had ever seen. Handmade of sparkling, clear quartz, it was rounded and polished till it shone like glass. Deep inside glowed a mystical red "star." A scarlet satin ribbon slipped through a small hole and transformed the pebble into a stunning necklace.

"W-Why, Aunt Kate!" she cried, throwing her arms around the older woman's plump neck. "It's spectacular! I'll treasure this always. I bet there's not another one like it in the whole wide world!"

"Well, reckon there is," her great-aunt corrected her matter-of-factly. "See, my pa done made two of them—one for me and one for my best friend."

As Granny tied the ribbon around Holly Jean's neck, her granddaughter asked, "Does your friend still have her necklace?"

Suddenly Aunt Kate turned grim. "No one knows, child. No one knows what evil befell poor, dear Maybelle White—her as married that wretched Max Morgan. Her as was killed in cold, cold blood." Pointing to Razorback Ridge, she cried, "Yes, her as haunts that mountain with her poor child to this very day!"

Chapter 10
Singing and Screaming

Remembering Maybelle Morgan's neglected grave down at the cemetery, Holly Jean stared at the older woman. "Y-You mean Madman Max's wife used to be your best friend?"

Aunt Kate smiled wistfully. "Like two peas in a pod, we was, Holly Jean. Your granny was still a shirttail young'un then, but me and Maybelle was already young ladies. The boys'd walk us home from prayer meetin' together. Ice cream socials and corn huskings too. Carriage rides—my, oh, my!

"Our mas even made us dresses out of the same pattern flour sacks—exact same size we was, you know. Maybelle's hair was firecracker-red like yours, while mine was gold as cornsilk. We sung duets together—good as anything you hear on the radio, and Maybelle played on a little mouth harp. Sounded for all the world like your own fancy little pipe."

"Flute, Aunt Kate."

"Whatever. Anyways, even after we growed up and she married that Morgan skunk, we was close. Named her girl-child after me, she did—little Daisy Katherine. The Daisy part's for flowers, of course. Maybelle was always plumb partial to flowers, you know—flowers and forest critters. Her little girl was too."

Suddenly Aunt Kate was sobbing. "Oh, it hurts so to think of poor Maybelle suffering now, wandering that lonely hill and crying for her pain to go away."

Granny reached for her sister's hand. "Now, now, Kate, the good Lord knows you loved Maybelle. He loves her, too, so you just forget them ghost stories. Them as loves Jesus sleeps in peace, not in suffering." She continued more crisply, "Your pa and me got a present for you too, Holly Jean. But you can't see it till we're back at the house."

Then she taught her granddaughter how to skip flat, round stones across the pond. Aunt Kate showed her how to blow on blades of grass to make sounds. After that Holly Jean splashed barefoot with Bear through the shallow side of the pond to catch crawdads.

At last Holly Jean plopped down to dry her feet and relax. She stretched out on the quilt and looked up at the rustling leaves. The smooth stones under the quilt felt warm on her back.

"You know, Granny," she confided, "this isn't the way I planned to celebrate my thirteenth birthday. But it's really been a fun day after all, thanks to you two!"

Of course, it would have been even more fun if Roger and Shirley had been there. And Aunt Bea and Papa Joe. Or if they'd all spent the day back in Cincinnati at the zoo, the museums, the big Coney Island amusement park or swimming pools—or just about *anywhere* but here!

That evening after a scrumptious dinner of pan-fried catfish, Granny and Kate cleaned up while Holly Jean started playing through her new songbook. The older women sang along joyfully to help her learn the music.

At last Aunt Kate exclaimed, "Why, this is good as camp meeting, Holly Jean! We sure miss having a guitar or piano played down at church. How about bringing your music pipe for services tomorrow? That would be a nice surprise for the folks."

Then she and Granny winked at each other. "And now I think your granny done got a surprise for you right here."

Granny stood up beside her kitchen cupboard. "What do you see on this here wall, Holly Jean?"

"Well, nothing, Granny, except the cupboard and your sunbonnet hook."

"Now, ain't that most peculiar? I see a door to a bedroom!"

Holly Jean was puzzled. "Where, Granny?"

Her little grandmother took a piece of cold, charred wood from the kitchen stove firebox and drew a big black *X* on the wall beside the cupboard. "Why, right about there, I reckon. You see it, too, Kate?"

Aunt Kate nodded. "Yep. Looks exactly like a door to a bedroom for a gal who's getting too big to sleep in the attic."

Holly Jean was mystified. "Why, Aunt Kate, you mean…? But how…?"

Granny laughed. "Your Papa Joe and me done decided to build you a little lean-to back here, child. Joe wants you to have a place to sleep warm and to study come school time. Bob Anderson'll start building soon's his corn's cultivated."

Holly Jean was awhirl with emotions—a room of her very own—what fun! She'd had to share her old one back in the city with Aunt Bea. And sleeping up in the low-ceilinged attic made dressing very awkward. But building that room seemed so final. Did that mean she was going to be stuck here in Hickory Hollow for years? Maybe *forever*?

That night she dreamed of skipping stones with Roger and showing Shirley how to fish. Except somehow they seemed to be putting *fish* on the hooks to catch *worms*! Then she dreamed of getting all dressed up in her best yellow dress and birthday sandals and starting off to meet Shirley and Roger and all her other friends at her old school.

Unfortunately, Cincinnati was a hundred miles away, and since she didn't have a ride, she had to walk. Soon her shoes fell apart; then her socks, but she kept on going. When she finally reached her old school and ran in through the school doors, however, she found herself right back in Granny's kitchen. All alone.

Waking with a pounding heart, Holly Jean sat straight up in her covers. Then she remembered: Today was Sunday, and she was going to play her flute at Granny's church—not as grand as doing a solo at her old school, of course, but better than nothing. At least it would make Granny and Aunt Kate happy, and it was something different to do.

Pulling on her everyday jeans, she grabbed her flute, new shoes, and a cotton dress to iron for church. Then she rushed barefoot down from the attic and across the yard to the porch.

Not paying attention as she hurried, she stepped into a pile of old dead holly leaves, their points against her bare skin as hard and sharp as needles. Hopping madly to get away from the leaves, she tripped—falling headlong into Grandpa Ned's climbing roses.

Instantly, her arms and legs were seized by dozens of thorns. Kicking desperately to free herself, Holly Jean knocked down a yellow jacket. Buzzing furiously, he sat right down on her big toe. And set it afire!

"Granny!" she screamed. "Aunt Kate! Help! *HELP!*"

Chapter 11
"On a Hill Far Away"

"Land o' Goshen!" her great-aunt exclaimed when she hobbled out to the porch to see what was going on. "Can't rightly decide whether to laugh or to cry!"

Aunt Kate and Granny pulled Holly Jean out of the rose bush, one thorn at a time. Then they carried her into the house—her arms and legs bleeding all over, her left foot already the size of a lunch bucket.

"Lawsy mercy, gal," her grandmother sighed. "Don't think I ever seed a more pitiful critter in all my born days!"

Granny Nanny carefully washed off the deep scratches and the red, swollen foot with cool well water. Aunt Kate covered them over with a soothing paste of baking soda and gave her some aspirin for the pain. Then they laid her down on a cool sheet in Aunt Kate's bed.

"Well, young lady, no church for you today," Aunt Kate announced. "Won't be no shoe on that foot for a week, neither, I reckon. But your scratches should be better by tomorrow."

"Think you can rest here a spell by yourself this morning?" Granny asked anxiously. "Me and Kate hates to go without you, but they's a special meeting today after morning service. We'd sure hate to let Brother Jake and Miss Linda down by not being there."

"I'll be fine," Holly Jean muttered drowzily. "Maybe I'll just sleep."

And thinking very sad thoughts, she did just that.

She awoke a few hours later to Bear's joyous barking when Granny and Aunt Kate returned. "What a great meeting!" Aunt Kate declared. "Never thought Morgan Mills folks would get around to it, but, by cracky, they're finally going to do something around here."

Holly Jean yawned and rubbed her eyes. "Do what, Aunt Kate?"

Aunt Kate took off her Sunday shoes and rubbed a bunion. "Why, have us a big Fourth of July wingding, that's what!"

"Amen!" Granny added cheerfully. "Brother Jake and Miss Linda both been after everyone to do something. So we all had us a little meeting today and decided to have a Fourth of July pie-and-music social up at the schoolhouse."

Aunt Kate loosened her sunbonnet strings. "To raise money for a new schoolhouse stove, Holly Jean. One they got now's so old we have to prop it up on one side with stones from the crick. Maybe we'll even have enough money left over to buy us hymnbooks for everyone at church to sing out of. Soon's we get them, we can have us a real revival meeting. Praise the Lord! Amen!"

Granny took off her own bonnet and tended to her granddaughter's wounds. "You'll enjoy the pie social, Holly Jean. There'll be young'uns from miles around, gals and fellers both, for you to meet. Why, we might get folks from as far away as Hog Flats and Cherokee Crossing."

Aunt Kate put on her apron. "Oh, Miss Linda asked about you, dear. Said she was sorry you couldn't play for us this week, but hopes you can next Sunday, Lord willing. Said if you brings your music pipe to play, she'll have a special surprise for you at church. Why, I ain't never seen that teacher-woman so all-fired up in all my born days!"

Holly Jean spent that night with her grandmother in Granny's narrow cot, almost swallowed up by its thick feather mattress.

"Sewed it myself, I did," Granny declared with pride. The blue and white striped ticking was secured with tiny, even stitches. She had made the cool, starched sheets and colorful quilts too.

Delightful as the bed was, though, Holly Jean didn't sleep a wink. The same deep scratches and hot, swollen foot that prevented her from climbing up to her attic room kept her tossing and turning all night long. Besides, the bed was too narrow to get comfortable in—especially with Granny there too. And after sleeping up in the airy attic, the cabin's tiny room seemed stifling.

But the next morning she felt well enough to sit out on the front porch, her sore foot propped up on Bear's back. Granny and Aunt Kate sat with her, snapping green beans and singing along as she practiced the hymns in her new book.

On Tuesday Holly Jean could hobble around the front yard with a broom for a cane. By Wednesday she could wear one of Aunt Kate's old shoes on her bad foot to weed the garden. But Aunt Kate was right; not until that Saturday did Jeannie's foot return to normal size. At last she was free!

All week long she had been planning for this moment. First on her list was to try to make friends with those darling barn kittens. Heading across the field with a pan of milk and some sausage scraps, she set them down on the barn floor. Then she plopped down on a hay bale to wait.

Soon she noticed one bright pair of eyes, then another. Suddenly four little kittens materialized, tumbling about, squealing with glee. Then four little noses twitched joyfully, as they scurried over to the pan. All at once the entire barn was alive with cats of every size and color—leaping from beams, rushing out of stalls—to join in the feast.

When the pan had been licked completely clean, the adult cats sat around washing their paws and whiskers. The kittens chased their tails. Now was the time for Holly Jean to try out her plan.

Breaking off a long straw, she dangled it near a black and white kitten. He began swatting at it and the other kittens joined in. Delighted, Holly Jean reached out to touch one.

Just like that, they all fled, hissing and squealing as if she'd tried to kill them! So much for making friends with *them*!

Next on her list was the falls—and its "ghost." With Bear and her flute in tow, she hiked slowly up to the lush ravine, trying to sort out her thoughts.

Aunt Kate had talked about *two* "ghosts"—Maybelle Morgan and her daughter, Daisy. But Holly Jean had only seen one. So was that Maybelle or Daisy? Or a different "ghost" altogether?

But, of course, ghosts didn't exist. She knew that from science class, and from church too. So maybe this "ghost" was just a shaft of light filtering down through the leafy canopy overhead.

Or just her imagination.

Settling down among the ferns, she rubbed Bear's long brown ears. "Guess you and me are having 'visions' like Aunt Kate, partner. Next thing you know we'll be having bad backs like her too. Then I'll have to rub you all over with horse liniment!"

She pulled out her flute and opened her music book to Aunt Kate's favorite, *The Old Rugged Cross.*

"Poor Maybelle Morgan loved it too," her great-aunt had said. "She loved Jesus, and she loved hills. She'd sit and sing, 'On a hill far away,' and they'd be tears in her eyes every single time. Why, reckon the only reason she married Max Morgan was 'cause his pa give him that farm up on a *hill.*"

Razorback Ridge, that is; the same hill Holly Jean was sitting on at this very moment!

As she finished the second verse, she heard an echo to her music—but not from across the hollow like a regular echo—no, from somewhere very near.

And not an exact duplicate of what she was playing, either. Sometimes the music ran a little ahead; sometimes a little behind, but it was obviously the very same tune.

A shiver ran up her spine. Who or what was making that "echo"? Mockingbirds? They were wonderful imitators, of course, but what wild bird knew *The Old Rugged Cross?*

Or was it the "ghost"?

Well, she refused to be scared, no matter what. She would keep right on playing, and let whoever or whatever was making that music come close enough for her to see who or what it was, once and for all.

During the third verse, the music did come nearer and nearer with each sweet note. Now she was sure that it wasn't a human voice, a flute echo, or even another flute.

No, and not a violin, piccolo, clarinet, or any other instrument Holly Jean knew. Not even a "mouth harp" or harmonica, such as Maybelle Morgan once played.

She strained to see something—anything! Then there it was, directly across from her, by a mulberry tree—something light and shiny and bright, playing *The Old Rugged Cross.*

On no instrument at all!

Holly Jean grabbed Bear and held the growling animal tightly between her knees to keep him from charging.

At that same instant, she heard something even more wonderful, but just as terrifying: a woman's voice singing, "And I'll cherish that old rugged cross." A voice as sweet and glorious as an angel's.

But a voice without a body!

Chapter 12
Concert at the Falls

As Holly Jean held her breath in wonder, the singer's body materialized. But it was hard to see either this musician or the other one through the dense trees and filtered light.

The one that made the sound of an instrument was about Holly Jean's height, with tangled white hair. In fact, he or she seemed to be white all over; but with one hand covering the mouth, she couldn't see the face.

The taller figure had long pale hair crowned with lacy white flowers, a flowing white gown, and a snow-white dove on one shoulder.

Holly Jean stopped playing in amazement, but the woman's sweet song continued, and so did the instrumental "echo."

Just then her knees turned to mush. Bear, no longer imprisoned between her legs, hurled himself free, and charged straight for the smaller music-maker.

Just like that both of them vanished. Completely.

Bear pawed frantically at the base of a boulder. She dropped her flute and ran after him. "What's the matter, boy?" she laughed nervously. "Think our ghosts turned into a rock?"

And then she saw it: a small, black pocket comb, very weathered and very worn.

And something else: footprints.

"Well, that settles it," she laughed to herself. "Ghosts don't use combs and leave footprints."

She slipped the comb into her jeans' pocket, whistled to Bear, and headed back to the falls, greatly relieved.

Until she realized something.

Anyone passing through these woods could have dropped that old comb—including her own father, Aunt Bea, or Uncle Tom when they were young. As for the footprints, she could have made them herself last time she came through here. So those clues still didn't prove anything about the "ghosts."

Back at the falls, Holly Jean started to pack up her flute. Then she noticed something tucked into her flute case: a long, dainty stem of Queen Anne's lace....

She shivered. "Bear, old boy, you and me are going to get to the bottom of this one of these days—or I'll eat my flute!"

Then Bear—to whom the word "eat" was the most marvelous word possible—yelped with delight, and raced her back down the hill.

Next morning on the way to church, Granny remarked, "Cat got your tongue, Holly Jean?"

Her granddaughter smiled. Truth to tell, her head was too full of thoughts to talk to anyone about them—thoughts of the two ghost-like musicians, the comb, the flower in her flute case. Of the solo she would have played at her school last week, and the one she would play this morning at church—of Roger, Shirley, Aunt Bea, and Papa Joe—of that very unkind Tootsie Anderson.

They could already hear that "surprise" by the time they crossed East Fork and headed up the road toward Morgan Mills.

"Lord love a duck!" Aunt Kate cried with astonishment. "I do believe someone's playing the church pianer!"

Someone very definitely was: a dark-haired young man with horn-rimmed spectacles and a serious face. Standing beside him was a glowing Miss Linda.

"Jeannie!" the teacher greeted her. "So glad your foot is better. I hope you can play for us this morning. Indeed, it's such a special occasion I invited my brother Tad along to play as well. He's a junior at Willow Bend High and accompanies the Glee Club there. Perhaps he can help you with your solo."

Holly Jean gave him a big smile and held out her hand. "Hello, Tad. I'm doing *Amazing Grace*—which I'm sure you already know backwards and forwards."

But he didn't even look up.

"This thing's a disgrace!" he grumped, banging on the piano. "Ten keys completely gone, and most of the ivory missing. No wonder nobody ever plays the dumb thing. You know, our church back in Willow Bend has a youth choir, an organ, and a grand piano. We've even got a bell ensemble and a small church orchestra."

Looking around, he shook his head in disgust. "But this place is, like, the pits."

To her, though, it looked a lot better than last time she was here. Two weeks ago, the only young people present were Tootsie and herself. Today Tootsie giggled on the back pew with several other teenagers. There were more adults here too, and a whole row of fidgeting children. Maybe word had gotten around about the visiting pianist, or Holly Jean's solo, or both.

Because there was still just the one hymnbook, Tad used it to play Brother Jake's selections. Holly was amazed at how well he performed, even with the piano in such poor condition. The congregation sang along with great enthusiasm, tapping and stomping their feet and shouting, "Hallelujah!" When the congregational singing was over, everyone clapped.

"Now that's the way we ought to be worshiping here every single Sunday!" Brother Jake exclaimed. "Miss Linda, you just invite that good-looking brother of yours to come back anytime he can, but especially for our big pie-and-music social. Why, if we can raise enough money for hymnbooks for everyone, maybe we'll have good singing like this here every week!"

After the offering, Holly Jean stood up for her solo. Tad, apparently expecting the worst, gave a halfhearted introduction. But when she started playing, his eyes lit up and he put his whole heart into the accompaniment.

After two verses, they stopped. But the music didn't. Instead, Aunt Kate stood up, arms lifted, tears flowing, and began singing the third verse without accompaniment. Then Granny joined her, then another worshiper and another, until the whole church was alive with the joy and wonder of the Lord.

"Hosanna!" shouted the pastor. "Why, when a preacher been lifted up to Glory like that he can't help but preach power!"

Unfortunately, much as Brother Jake loved God and His Word, his sermons droned on and on, like flies on a hot, sticky day. And despite his earnest plea, no one came forward during his invitation at the end of the service.

Afterwards, Tootsie and her friends crowded around Tad.

"Oooo, you play so good!" Tootsie cooed. "You just gotta come back Fourth of July and play for our pie social. Me'n the rest of us young folks gonna sing *This World Is Not My Home*. Grandpappy Bob and the Men's Quartet will do *Just a*

Little Talk with Jesus. My brother Andy gonna play his guitar, with my sister Annie Sue on the musical saw. We're gonna have us a banjo too. So we'd just love to have you on the piano."

No mention, of course, of Holly Jean or her flute.

Tad smiled vacantly at Tootsie and her friends, then turned back to Holly Jean.

"Wow! Where did you learn to play like that, girl? We could sure use you in our high school orchestra. Look, I'll come play at the pie social if you will. What would you like for us to play there?"

Blushing, she thought of the sheet music Roger had given her before she left. "What about *God Bless America*?"

"Good choice. It's patriotic, and even these country bumpkins have probably heard it. Maybe we can get together before then to practice. What do you say?"

She laughed. "Sounds like fun." Turning to Tootsie, she added, "Would your group like to practice with us?"

Tootsie fluttered her eyelashes. "Why, I'd practice with Tad Wilson anytime. Music, and anything else he wants!" Then, giggling, she left with her friends.

Aunt Kate walked back home with her arm around Holly Jean. "My, my," she exclaimed, "we was both so proud of you this morning, girl. Ain't had no idea you could make such fine music on that-there pipe."

"Well, Aunt Kate," she replied, "I didn't realize how well you could sing, either. You got the whole congregation stirred up. Why don't you practice a solo for the pie social? Or you and Granny do a duet?"

Her great-aunt laughed in protest. "An old woman like me?" But she beamed with pleasure.

Just then, Holly Jean remembered the ghostly singer on the hillside. "Aunt Kate, when you saw that 'ghost' up on Razorback Ridge, did it sing to you? Or say anything?"

"Now, Holly Jean!" Granny exploded. "What you bringing that up for? Ain't no such thing as ghosts. You know that."

But her great-aunt looked sadly up at the hill. "Yes, I was hearing her singing, Holly Jean. Singing *The Old Rugged Cross*. I started singing along with her, like we used to do, and she come closer and closer. Then I sees her red hair done turned white as death down in that cold, cold grave."

"'Oh, Maybelle!' I cried. 'What can I do to ease your sorrow?' But she just screamed an unearthly scream and disappeared. *And there wasn't nothing I could do for her!*"

As her great-aunt wiped her eyes, Holly Jean asked, "Aunt Kate, didn't you say Maybelle liked flowers?"

"Law, chile, she loved them. She and Daisy both. Always had the growingest hollyhocks and sweetpeas in the county. Once gave me a begonia cutting. I got that plant to this very day. But she favored wildflowers best—daisies, of course, black-eyed Susans, and Queen Anne's lace."

Queen Anne's lace? Holly Jean shuddered and changed the subject. "Do people really take pies to pie socials, Granny?"

"'Deed they do, child. Apple pies, blackberry, gooseberry, lemon, chocolate, pumpkin, mince, butterscotch—every kind you can imagine. Pan pies and cobblers both."

"Aunt Bea used to make wonderful blackberry cobblers,"

Holly Jean remembered. "We'd eat them hot with lots of milk or whipped cream."

Granny chuckled. "And so can we—this very day! Holly Jean, when we git home, fetch us some blackberries from up at pasture. Me 'n Kate'll fix you a dessert the likes of which you won't never find again this side of the Pearly Gates!"

After lunch, Holly Jean changed into her jeans. Then with a bucket and Bear, she headed up the road.

Each year Uncle Tom had a big field of corn planted for Granny. Because the soil was thin up in the hollow, every year the corn was planted in a different field, leaving all the others fallow, or unused, till the next year. Left unplowed, the fields grew plenty of wild grass and clover for Morgie and Star, and blackberries for anyone willing to pick them.

Part of the pasture fence was barbed wire, part split rail. Holly Jean moved the top rail off one section, then she and Bear scampered over into the "briar patch." Across the field by the creek, Granny's mule and cow rested side by side in the shade, tails swatting each other's flies.

Running across the field to them, Holly Jean gave both animals a good scratching and some juicy green leaves; then she started picking berries. The sun was hot, the berries squishy, the thorns painful, the rocks underfoot uncomfortable. As she made her way around the field, the berries in her bucket piled higher and higher. Only her fingers were busy with berries while her mind was busy with other things—Roger, Tad, Shirley, Tootsie, and the two "ghosts" up by the falls.

Then a cry cut through her daydreams.

It was old Morgie—screaming in terror. Something white was there beside him, right against the barbed wire fence. *One of the "ghosts!"*

This time she had no hesitation. It was time to end all these mysteries. "Come on, boy," she yelled to Bear. "Go sic 'em, kid! And don't let go!"

Chapter 14
Caught in a Briar Patch

Bear hurled himself across the field, dashing around the larger bushes and leaping over the smaller ones. Holly Jean scrambled after him, ripping her jeans on the briars, desperate to reach the "ghost" before it disappeared.

But it didn't even move. Instead, it seemed to cower under the trees by the creek, cringing against the fence.

She approached the creature cautiously. Even with rather longish hair, "it" appeared to be a "he"—indeed, a boy a little younger than she was.

But how strange he looked! A pale straw hat sat atop tangled locks of purest white. His face and bare arms were as colorless as his shirt, while his eyes seemed carved from ice. Even his overalls had faded completely.

Not a ghost. Not a fairy. But a human boy with no pigment, no color, in his skin or hair—such as Holly Jean had studied about in science last year. An *albino,* as pale as could be.

She almost laughed in relief. "Down, Bear!" she ordered.

But instead of running away as before, or standing up and

talking to her, the boy continued to huddle, his hands over his face.

"P-Please, Grandma Maybelle!" he begged hysterically. "D-Don't hit me. Ma 'n me just missed you. We wanted to follow you and watch you and listen to your purty music. We didn't mean to hurt you none or make you mad."

Holly Jean stared at him. She had thought *he* was a ghost. And here he thought that *she* was one!

"N-No, no," she stammered. "Look, I'm just a girl. Holly Jean Roberts. Why would you think I was your grandmother's ghost?"

He lifted his eyes a little, his anguish still evident. "That red hair. That music. T-That 'fairy stone.'"

"Oh. Look, I can explain everything, but first maybe you'd like something back."

She handed him the comb she had found on Razorback Ridge. As his eyes lit up with recognition, Holly Jean said, "Now you can comb your hair."

Then she saw why he hadn't fled: his thick, white hair was caught on the barbed wire fence. In a moment she had him free.

"Combin's for sissies," he retorted, standing up. Then, reaching into his pocket, he pulled out a piece of waxed paper, and held both it and the comb to his lips. Out flowed *The Old Rugged Cross*.

So that was this stranger's "unearthly" instrument. He had been playing a *comb!*

Holly Jean giggled. "So now do you believe that I'm Nan Roberts' granddaughter, and not your grandmother's ghost?"

He nodded slowly. "Well, maybe. See, we seed you down there at Miz Nanny's farm, but we didn't know if you was a ghost or not. Ma said if you looked any more like Grandma did when she was young, you'd have to be twins. We used to listen to you singing out when you was pulling weeds in the garden. I declare, you sounded just like Grandma Maybelle."

Holly Jean stared at him. "How could you hear me from way up on the ridge? Why, that must be a mile or two away."

He giggled. "Sound always carries up; didn't you know that? Up there we can hear might near everything in the valley."

"Oh." Suddenly, she was embarrassed to think of some of the things she said that this boy might have heard. "Well, then it's settled. I'm Holly Jean Roberts. I used to live in the city, but now I live with Granny and Aunt Kate down the road apiece. This is our pasture. That's Morgie the mule, named after your grandfather, and Star the cow. And this is Granny's dog, Bear. What's your name?"

"Moon. For Moonbeam."

"Moonbeam what? What's your last name?"

He sighed. "Don't rightly know, Miss Holly Jean. Ma won't tell me. She keeps Pa's picture under her mattress, but Grandpa Max don't know nothin' about it. Grandpa says if he ever saw my pa again he'd kill him for sure."

"Why?"

Moon shrugged. "Don't know that either. Why are you staring at me?"

Holly Jean blushed. "I'm sorry. I guess I'm still so surprised to see you and know you're real and not a ghost. Why are you staring at me?"

Moon grinned. "Ain't never seed a gal before. Leastways, not up close. I mean, besides Ma and Grandma. Do all girls look like you?"

Her mouth flew open. "You've never seen a girl before? Not even at school?"

"Ain't never been to no school or nothin'. Grandpa won't let me. Ma says the farm's more fun, anyhow—'specially the woods. 'Cause here we can climb trees and chase squirrels and find hickory nuts and ginseng. And swing over the creek on a grapevine."

Holly Jean decided she liked this strange boy. "Here, have some blackberries," she offered. "Where's that grapevine?"

"It's up where the hollow narrows. I can swing from our ridge clear over to the other one. That's how I get down here to pick dewberries."

"Dewberries? Not blackberries?"

He looked away, embarrassed. "Dewberries is in the shade; blackberries in the sun."

"Oh." Of course, people with an albino condition could get terrible sunburns. Bright light hurt their eyes too.

Suddenly, she spilled out her pent-up questions: "Moon, was that your mother singing up at the falls with you? How old are you? And how did your grandma die?"

"Yes, that was Ma. Don't she sing fine? I've got twelve years now, I reckon. And I don't know how Grandma died. Ma won't say, and Grandpa won't talk about it."

"Oh." So much for that.

She tried again. "Look, I'm very sorry you never got to go to school. This fall I'll be going to school at Morgan Mills for the very first time myself. Maybe we can talk your grandfather into letting you come too. Miss Linda Wilson's the teacher. She's very pretty and very nice. It would be good for you to meet other boys and girls."

Then she remembered the Morgan Mills church. "And you and your mother are welcome to go along to church with us Sundays too. Your grandpa too, if he wants. They're going to have a big pie-and-music social down at the schoolhouse on the Fourth of July to buy a new school stove and maybe some hymnbooks. It sounds like a lot of fun."

Moon scratched his head. "Ain't never been to no meetinghouse of no kind, Miss Jeannie. Ma used to go, but not since Grandma died. She told me what it's like, though. Sure sounds fun, the music and all. Ma sings me church songs all the time. She reads to me from the Good Book too."

Grinning, he added, "And I sure loves me some good pie. Can't think of nothing nicer'n eating pie with you, Miss Holly Jean. 'Cept maybe eatin' fried chicken and pie both!

"But," he continued dejectedly, "Grandpa don't hold no truck with lowlander folk no more. Not since Grandma died. He says if Ma or me goes down off the hill, he'll beat us for sure. Why, if he knew I was talking to you—Lordy!" Jumping up, Moon said, "Look, I'd better go. Can I see you again soon?"

She thought a moment. "We'll need a secret signal," she decided, "so no one will find out we're talking to each other. How about the song, *In the Garden?* You know: 'I come to the garden alone'? We can sing or play it as a signal to meet at the falls."

Moon giggled. "You're sure fun to know, Miss Holly Jean Roberts. You're the best friend I ever had. Onliest one too, of course, 'ceptin' for Ma and my hound dog, Bones. And my possum, Pete. And my 'coon, Mischief. And my cat, Scratch. And my pet crow, Screech. And of course, old Skitters, my lizard. Here, have my dewberries; I ate too many of yours."

He dumped his bucket into hers. Then he grinned. "Sure proud to know you, Miss Holly Jean Roberts."

And just like that he vanished.

Holly Jean stood staring at the spot where Moon had disappeared. Then girl and dog rounded up mule and cow, and headed on back home with the berries.

Granny was thrilled at her bucket. "Lawsy, did you ever see such plump dewberries, Kate? Them'll make cobblers and a quart of preserves too."

Kate put on her blue apron with the red rickrack edges. "I'll take over the cobbler, Nan. You and Holly Jean go a-bikin'."

Holly Jean stared at them both. "Biking?"

Granny nodded firmly. "Your pa done brought your cycle with you, now, didn't he, Holly Jean? Always wanted to learn how to ride one of them contraptions. Figure I might as well start now, since I ain't never going to get no younger."

Holly Jean swallowed hard. "Uh, well, sure, Granny." She wheeled her bike out of the corncrib where Papa Joe had stored it, onto a level spot on the road. "Now get on and I'll show you how to pedal."

Granny shook her head. "Lawsy, no. You get on first and let me watch, so I can get the hang of it. Then I'll try."

Only three weeks before, Holly Jean had ridden her bike along wide, flat, well-paved streets. This road was narrow, steep, bumpy, rocky, and full of ditches. It took some getting used to, but finally she was able to ride up and down the rutted dirt road without pitching over. "See, Granny?"

"Got it!" Granny exclaimed. "Now it's my turn!"

Holly Jean helped her get on. "All right, this is the handlebar. Hold on tight to it with both hands and turn it the way you want to go. These are the pedals. You push them with your feet to go. When you want to stop, just move your feet backward on the pedals. Like this."

Granny Nanny was so short she could hardly sit and pedal at the same time. So Holly Jean ran alongside her, holding the bike erect.

Aunt Kate came out to watch. She laughed so much she had to wipe her eyes with her apron. "Now ain't that a sight?" she chortled. "Sure wished I had me a Brownie camera right now!"

"You shut up, Kate!" Granny yelled. "Get yourself on back inside and don't let that cobbler burn."

As soon as Aunt Kate left, Granny said, "Now, I want to try without you a-holding on."

Reluctantly, Holly Jean let go. With determination, her grandmother headed up the hill, wobbling precariously from side to side. Then she got off, turned the bike around, and got back on again. Then down the hill she came.

"I'm doing it, Holly Jean!" she squealed. "Hey, Bear! Look at Granny, boy!"

Yelping with confused delight, the giant dog came bounding up the road toward her, as she bounced downhill, faster and faster.

Till she hit a rock.

Her granddaughter saw it all in slow motion—the rock, the bike, the dog—Granny flying over the handlebars and right up into the air.

"Aunt Kate!" she screamed. "Come quick! Granny might be hurt real bad!"

Aunt Kate rushed out of the house—just in time to see Granny and Bear tumble into the iris bed as the bike rolled right on down to the creek.

"Granny!" Holly Jean screamed, running to her. "Are you all right?"

Her grandmother sat up, dazed. She felt her arms, her legs, her back. "Well, I'm a mite banged up, but don't think I cracked no bones."

Breaking into a joyous smile, Granny yelled, "But I did it, Kate! I did it! Did you see me going down that hill lickety-split—like a cat with its tail on fire? Can't wait to do it again, I can't!"

Chapter 16
Dreaming by the Fire

This time it was Granny who was half-dragged, half-carried back to the house. Aunt Kate and Holly Jean rubbed her bruises with liniment and bandaged up her skinned knee. Even poor Bear, rather the worse for having Granny land on top of him, came in for some tender, loving care.

While Holly Jean retrieved her bike, Aunt Kate made Granny some soothing sassafras tea. Then she brought out bowls full of steaming blackberry cobbler piled high with frothy whipped cream.

Granny rested her bowl on her propped-up leg. "Living don't come better than this!" she giggled.

Her sister frowned. "Laws a-mercy, Nan Roberts! Way you was a-going, you might not have been living much longer, period!"

That evening out on the porch, Aunt Kate spit on her finger and held it up to the air. "Wind shifting," she decided. "Smells like rain. I thought I felt my rheumatism a-coming on."

"Why don't we listen to the radio and find out for sure?" Holly Jean asked.

"Ha! Don't you think *my* bones can tell the weather just as good as some city slicker announcer?"

But after Holly Jean helped her great-aunt milk the cow—Granny being the one sitting home this time—Aunt Kate relented. They turned on the large wooden radio, rounded on top like a church window, and listened to *Jack Benny, Fred Allen*, and *Amos 'n Andy*. Granny laughed until she got the hiccups.

Next came lots of dreamy music. Then the war news. The bloody battle of Midway had finally been won. The Germans were bombarding Russia with bombs, while in North Africa, America's allies were on the run.

"Makes me think of poor little Willie," Granny sighed. "Joe too. Lord, I hope they come home safe. God bless all them poor boys."

Last of all came the weather report: "Cloudy, with 40% chance of rain."

But the next morning the sky was a glorious red. "See, Aunt Kate," Holly Jean pointed out, "it's not going to rain, after all."

But her great-aunt shook her head. "Red skies at night: sailors' delight," she quoted. "But, 'Red skies at morning: sailors give warning.' Thar's a storm coming for sure, so we'd better get our chores done fast as we can afore it hits."

Holly Jean was amazed at how quickly her great-aunt could move when she had a mind to. They brought in fresh water, fed the chickens and hogs, checked for eggs, and shut the chickens up in the henhouse. Then Holly Jean pitched plenty of hay for Morgie and Star, while Aunt Kate milked the cow. There'd be no going to pasture for the animals today.

Afterward, Aunt Kate poured a little of the fresh milk into a pan. Instantly, cats appeared from everywhere. They still wouldn't let Holly Jean touch them, but after they ate, the little black and white kitten sat on one of her shoes and played with her shoelace.

Right then she decided to name him Domino. "It sure takes a long time to make friends with these cats, doesn't it, Aunt Kate?" she sighed.

Aunt Kate chuckled. "Lawsy, child, you've only been here two weeks. I'd say you were doing right pert, myself."

Only two weeks? It seemed more like two *years!*

While they were in the barn, the wind had built up to gale force, bending huge trees almost horizontal. It took all their strength to push against the barn door to get out. Clinging tightly to the fence and to each other to keep from being toppled over, they fought their way back to the house.

Once there, they bolted the shutters tight. Granny set a bucket on the kitchen floor under a spot where the roof always leaked. Then they built a roaring fire in the fireplace and lit the kerosene lamp. Even Bear was brought inside for safety.

The fireplace hadn't been used since early spring. "What's that sizzle?" Holly Jean asked, listening to the chimney.

Granny winked. "Probably fried copperhead snakes."

"For Heaven's sake, Nan!" her sister protested. "Don't you pay her no mind, Holly Jean. That's just the rain a-starting to sprinkle on our metal roof."

Soon the sprinkles turned to drops, and the drops to great sheets of rain. Aunt Kate rocked contentedly. "That-there's a shower of blessing, I reckon. We can sure use the water."

Granny pulled out some mending to do. Sprawled on a rag rug beside them, Holly Jean cuddled up next to Bear and stared into the fireplace. She seemed to see her father's red hair in the crimson flames.

"I sure miss Papa Joe and Aunt Bea," she sighed.

Her grandmother patted her head. "Now don't you fret, child. There's probably letters from both of them a-waiting us down at Tom's. Soon as the rain's over and the crick's down, you can take a run down there and see."

"You mean you expect the creek to flood?"

"Not really flood; it'll just be too high to cross on foot."

Holly Jean leaned against her grandmother's knee. "Granny, how old are you?"

Granny Nanny laughed. "Why, how old do you think I am, child? Here, figure it out: I was seventeen when I married your Grandpa Ned, and Kate here was twenty-two. I was eighteen when Tom was born. Twenty when your pa came along. And thirty when I had Bea."

Then if Papa Joe was now thirty-four.... "You mean you're fifty-four?"

"Sounds old to you, don't it, Holly Jean? But inside I still feel frisky as a spring chicken. Why, your great-great-grand-pa Ebenezer Roberts what built this here cabin lived to be ninety-seven! I ain't nowhere near that yet."

Holly Jean looked at Aunt Kate. "And you're fifty-nine?"

Aunt Kate chuckled. "When my rheumatism hits, I'm a hundred. But when I meet some fine figure of a man my age, I turn sixteen again. I had boyfriends once too, you know."

"Who did you go out with, Aunt Kate?"

Her great-aunt sat up straighter in her chair and smiled into the fire. "Well, now, me'n Maybelle was always squired to prayer meetings by Hershell Morgan's boys. Maybelle'n me sung duets at church-meetings, see. Sometimes the four of us did quartets. I was so proud to be going out with such an up-and-coming feller. And Jake had such fine black hair."

"You mean Brother Jake, the preacher at church?" Holly Jean tried to imagine the stooped minister as ever being young, or his thin silver hair once being as thick and black as Tad's. "So you double-dated with Maybelle and Madman Max?"

"Even went in Jake's pa's carriage to camp meetings over to Pine Lick. Finest carriage in the county it was too. Real leather. Hershell Morgan was well-off in those days, you know. Highly thought of too. People brought their grain and lumber to his mills from miles around. Raised fine crops of corn and soybeans on his bottom-land farm, and mules up on his hilltop land—the farm he give to Max. Why, people bought his fine mules from far away as Lexington."

Aunt Kate's face was soft in the firelight. "Jake's pa was partial to me, you know. Always called me 'Jake's Kitten Kate' and treated me like a daughter. Ah, those were the days."

Holly Jean was touched. "But if you were in love with Brother Jake, Aunt Kate, why did you break up with him?"

Just then thunder rolled from mountain to mountain and lightning split the sky—so bright it shone right through the cracks in the shutters.

"No!" Aunt Kate shouted, suddenly banging her fist. "No! I ain't never loved no man and never will. And don't you forget it!"

Then her head slumped forward, her great chest heaved, and she wailed like a broken-hearted child.

Chapter 17
White Cliffs and
Long White Gowns

Because of the storm, Holly Jean spent that night in Granny's bed again. The rain pounding on the metal roof soon lulled her off to sleep. By morning, however, a brilliant sun sprayed rainbows over every sparkling leaf. The storm was over, and the sky once more blue and clear.

Their little creek was a different story, though. Usually shallow and placid, it now churned deep and yellow and angry, tumbling down the hollow with astonishing ferocity.

The next day, though, it was back to normal. Large puddles still covered part of the pasture and cornfield. A car or cow that slid off the road might find itself deep in mud, but at least the old dirt road was once more passable.

Almost crazy with "cabin fever," Holly Jean could hardly wait to try walking out to Uncle Tom's store. So as soon as Granny gave her the weekly shopping list, she pulled on her rain boots. Then she and Bear tore off down the road, splashing happily through the stream.

At last she reached the end of her hollow. There the waters of East Fork, by the old mill ruins, were still swift and deep. The only way she could cross the stream now was on an ancient, little-used footbridge, its creaking planks suspended precariously by wires over the roaring water.

Terrified she would pitch right off into the torrents, she held tightly to the wires as she crossed—almost paralyzed with fear. Bear, however, plunged right into the water and swam to the other side, where he blithely shook half the creek all over her!

When they reached her uncle's store, Whitey the cat hissed at Bear from the windowsill. Then the dog plopped down outside to wait for her. Inside, the store was dark and cool, with ribbons of flypaper hanging everywhere.

"Well, howdy there, Miss Holly Jean!" her uncle called. "Here, get yourself a root beer and some peanuts. Then you and me's going to have ourselves a real checker game."

He drew up a nail keg and two orange crates. They laid the checkerboard across the keg and sat on the crates. "Now which do you want—black or red?" he asked.

Holly Jean laughed. "Red, of course, to match my hair."

"Then firecracker-red it is." And he proceeded to lay the pieces out on the board and explain the game to her.

Just then Aunt Tillie came into the store from the living quarters behind it, glowing with joy. "Miss Holly Jean!" she cried. "We just got a letter from our little Willie! Let me read it to you!"

"Little Willie" was over six feet tall, but Aunt Tillie had called him "little" for so long, it seemed to be part of his name. Her aunt pulled up a pickle barrel to sit on and started to read:

Dear folks,

I sure miss you all. I can't tell you where I am, but we've had a lot of action here in the Pacific. Seems like I'm a million miles away. Seen all the ocean ever I want to see. Tell Holly Jean hello for me.

And ask that Annie Sue Anderson if she's gotten a broken arm. Ain't got no letter from that gal for over a month now. First thing you know, I'm gonna think she's gotten sweet on some-one else.

Well, gotta go git this war over with. Then I can come back home to the good old U.S.A. and eat some of Mom's fried potatoes. And beat you at checkers, Pop.

Love, Willie

Aunt Tillie dabbed at her eyes. Uncle Tom turned his head away and blew his nose. Holly Jean felt so sorry for them both—their only child thousands of miles away in such terrible danger.

Trying to comfort them, she said, "Willie sure writes a good letter, Aunt Tillie. Maybe by the time he comes home I'll play checkers well enough to beat him myself!" Uncle Tom laughed heartily at that, but his eyes were still red. And he seemed too sad to finish the game.

Holly Jean walked over to the Post Office corner. "Any mail for Granny or Aunt Kate or me, Aunt Tillie?"

"Letter from your pa. Looks like he's still at Fort Knox, and one from Bea. Always said she had the fanciest handwriting ever I done see. Be sure and let me know what she says. Hope she likes her new place. And this big envelope's for you, Miss Holly Jean. Be mighty proud to know what's in it."

Glancing at Roger's address in the corner, she pretended not to hear. She didn't plan to share Roger with anyone—especially not her gossipy aunt!

But she did want her aunt to share some gossip about someone else. "Aunt Tillie, is Brother Jake married?"

"Him? Ha! Confirmed old bachelor man that one is. Just as well, I suppose. He could never support no family on what little comes in from offerings. Biggest amount I ever saw in the plate on a Sunday was $5.43—and that was on foot-washing day, seven years ago! Sometimes all he gits is a tough old rooster or maybe a sack of potatoes.

"Why, that poor man'd starve to death iffen he didn't farm a little on the side. But he never gives up, you know. Says God called him to preach and he can't never turn his back on God."

"Didn't he and Aunt Kate used to go together?"

"Well, reckon they did. Afore my time, of course. But then they split up, and she went her way and he went his'n, and now she's a spinster lady. Now that's just life sometimes, ain't it?"

Uncle Tom wrapped up Granny's order with brown butcher paper and string. "By the way, girl, Bob Anderson said he'll build your room soon's the ground's dry enough. I asked Mr. Bob to fix the roof up good too. No sense having a new room with an old, leaky roof over it.

"And tell that ma of mine to stay away from her cornfield. I know that woman—always loves to cultivate after a good rain. I'll get a hired man up there next week to do it for her. Tarnation! Can't keep that woman down nohow."

But when Holly Jean reached home, cultivating her corn was exactly what Granny was doing.

"*Swing low, sweet chariot,*" she boomed at the top of her lungs, as she guided her patient old mule between rows of young field corn.

"Gee, Morgie!" she called, pulling the reins to the right. Then at the end of each row, "Haw, boy!"—pulling them to the left.

Holly Jean set the groceries and letters down in the kitchen. She could see Aunt Kate out in the garden, cutting rhubarb. Holly would love to know what Papa Joe and Bea wrote, but the letters were addressed to all three of them, so she'd have to wait till Granny and Aunt Kate were free to read them.

She looked up at the hillside behind the house. The waterfall must be something to see after all that rain.

"Come on, boy," she called to Bear. "Let's go take a hike. I can play my flute up there and read my letter from Roger."

A short while later, after a damp climb through sodden leaves and dripping branches, she spread out a towel on the moist moss and sat down. Bear immediately deserted her to chase a frog.

First she opened the large envelope from Roger. Inside was sheet music for *White Cliffs of Dover*, and a note:

Dear Red:
Heard this song last week, and it reminded me of us being apart. So I got a flute and trumpet duet of it down at

the music shop. Maybe if you practice the flute part and I work on the trumpet one, we could play it next time we see each other. Well, got to study for end-of-school exams. See how lucky you were to move before exams started? Shirley says to say hi.

  Your friend, Roger

She sat dreaming for a minute of Roger's grin and the cute way his nose turned up at the end. *All right, Roger, I'll learn this stupid music and we will play that duet. I don't know when, but sometime! Maybe we can even get Tad Wilson to play along with us!*

Then she opened the music and tried the first notes: "There'll be bluebirds over the white cliffs of Dover…."

Bluebirds were for happiness. She remembered that from all the Saturday afternoon matinees and cartoons she and Shirley used to see together. Aunt Kate once knew happiness too, but now just thinking about Brother Jake made her very sad. What would the future bring for Holly Jean— happiness and love and fame? Or just being stuck forever up this lonesome hollow?

She gave a loud sigh.

"Oh, don't be sad, Miss Holly Jean!"

Startled speechless, she dropped her flute. Instantly, Moon was there beside her.

"W-Where did you come from?" she stammered.

Grinning, he pointed. "Up that-there tree. I was a-watching you. You're fun to watch, Miss Holly Jean."

"Well, it's not polite to watch someone when they don't know it, Moon! People need their privacy."

He smiled sweetly. "Why? I've been waiting for you to play *In the Garden*, Miss Holly Jean, like you promised."

"But it was raining, Moon. It was too wet to come."

"Not for me. I like it when it rains. Then there's no sunshine to have to stay out of. I can run through the fields and splash in the creek and keep my eyes open as wide as I want."

He pointed to Roger's note. "Is that a happy letter?"

"Well, yes. It's from a friend of mine back in the city. His name is Roger. He likes music too. He sent me this music to play."

Moon stared at the sheet music. "Why, hit's just a piece of paper with flyspecks all over it. That's not music. Music's inside." And he pointed to his heart.

She laughed. "Yes, but these are very special kinds of flyspecks, Moon. When I look at them it's called 'reading music.' Like Roger's letter is 'reading words.'"

Moon stared off in the distance. "Ain't never read nothin'. It all looks like hen-scratching to me." He smiled. "But I liked watching you when you was reading, Miss Holly Jean. You're sure pretty when you're thinking like that."

Jeannie blushed. "Look, Moon, we've got to get you to school so you can learn to read too. If we can find out what happened to your Grandma Maybelle and your father, I think your grandpa will quit being so mad and let you come to school. Your mother could be such a big help, if only she would trust me!"

Just then a long white gown fluttered down from overhead, followed by flowing white hair and a stream of soft white blossoms that landed directly in front of Holly Jean.

Moon's mother smiled a mystical, faraway smile. "Of course I trust you, love," she said sweetly, fondling the "fairy stone" necklace around her neck.

Her voice was full of longing. "But, Ma, we's all getting so tired of you a-being dead. Why don't you just come on back home?"

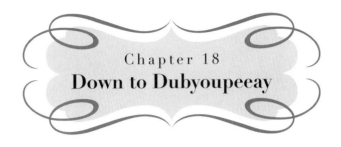

The last time Holly Jean saw Moon's mother, she thought Daisy was a ghost. Now, apparently Moon's mother thought *she* was one—the ghost of Maybelle Morgan!

"D-Daisy," she replied hesitantly, "you miss your ma a lot, don't you? Well, I want to help you—help you and Moon and your father too. Would you like to talk about it?"

"Sure, Ma." Daisy's long tresses were so pale it was hard to tell whether they were the blonde of youth or the silver of old age.

She peered curiously at Holly Jean. "Glad to see your broke neck's all better now. You're shorter'n you used to be, but I reckon being dead does that to a body. Having to fit in the coffin and all. Anyways, you still make sweet music like always."

Putting her arm around her son, Daisy said, "See how big Moon done growed? Ain't he the shiningest fairy child as ever you saw, white as a trillium flower in springtime? Helps Pa around the farm like a man now, he does. Won't make you climb up no haylofts after him no more, neither, Ma. So it's all safe for you to come home."

Moon gasped, his face twisted in horror, but Daisy didn't notice. "It'll all be just like it used to be, Ma. You 'n Pa 'n me 'n Ben 'n little Moon. And no more problems never again."

And she held out her arms to Holly Jean.

Holly Jean's head was suddenly spinning. Was Moon's grandmother killed by falling from a hayloft and breaking her neck? And was Moon somehow to blame, instead of his grandfather? And what about this "Ben"? Was he Daisy's long-missing husband?

She took the woman's hand. "Want Ben to come home too, Daisy?"

"Oh, yes'm, more'n anything in the world. But he's gone down the mountain to Dubyoupeeay and ain't got back home yet. Hope he'll bring Moon 'n me some pretties when he comes. Maybe a new red ribbon for my fairy stone, just like your'n, Ma!"

Suddenly she stopped. "Oh, law! Left them beans a-boiling and they'll be burnt for sure! I'll put some cornbread on for you too, Ma! You always did take a shine to my cornbread. Now, y'all come, y'hear?"

And she vanished.

Moon was still trembling.

"Now I remember!" he moaned. "I'm a-going up the loft after my kitty Scratch. And Grandma's a-calling, but I don't pay her no mind. So she comes up after me. And…oh, now I do remember, Miss Holly Jean! I do remember!"

She put her arm around his shoulders. "There, there, Moon, it wasn't your fault. Besides, that was a long time ago. Your grandma is happy with God now. The ones we need to help are you and your mother and grandfather. Do you think your father's name might be Ben?"

He sniffled. "Don't rightly know. I just called him Pa. I wasn't more'n four or so when he done took off, but I sure liked him. He'd carry me 'round on his shoulders and.... Well, lawsy, I sure miss him, Miss Holly Jean. Miss him a lot."

"Why does your mother call you a 'fairy child'?"

"'Cause I'm so pale. Everyone knows fairies is pale as moonlight. That's why Ma named me Moonbeam. She said I was too precious to share with the world. Said they wouldn't understand, and they'd laugh at my white skin and hair or be skeert of me. Some folks is skeert of fairies and spirits and such like, you know.

"But I'm glad you're not skeert of me, Miss Holly Jean," and he smiled shyly through his tears.

Well, that explained why no one in Morgan Mills even knew Moon existed. "Of course, I'm not afraid of you, Moon. But we do have some serious work ahead of us, if we're going to find your father. First, we've got to locate this 'Dubyoupeeay'—wherever that is—and see if he's still there. I think once your daddy comes home, your grandpa will quit being so mad. Then you can come to church and school with me and the other boys and girls."

She thought of Miss Linda and Tad there in the county seat of Willow Bend. Papa Joe said there was a library there, a courthouse, even a newspaper office. No one at Morgan Mills seemed to know anything about Moon's father. But if Ben really did live on the Morgan farm for four or five years, there should be a record of him *somewhere*.

Of course, they didn't know Ben's last name. But if they knew what he looked like....

"Moon, remember that picture you said your mother kept under her mattress? Do you think you could slip it out long enough for me to show to Miss Linda, the teacher? I think maybe she can help us find your father."

He was quiet for a moment. "It won't be easy, Miss Holly Jean," he said at last. "But I'll do it for you and for my sweet ma, even if Grandpa kills me!"

Then he vanished too.

Chapter 19
Letters of Love

Back at the cabin, Holly Jean helped Aunt Kate make a crust for her rhubarb pie. Soon Granny unhitched old Morgie for a well-deserved rest from his plowing, and headed home as well.

"Ah, that rhubarb sure smells good!" Nan Roberts called from the washpan stand by the kitchen door. "Holly Jean, ain't no one in this whole county makes rhubarb pies good as Kate does. They's even better'n her lemon ones."

"Which kind are you going to bake for the pie social, Aunt Kate?" Jeannie asked.

"Which kind would you like me to make for you, Holly Jean?"

"No, not for me—for yourself. Aren't you taking a pie too?"

Her great-aunt chuckled. "Land o' mercy, chile! An old lady like me? Now wouldn't that be a sight? Ain't no one would bid on it. Why, there's only one old bachelor-man in these parts I even know of!"

Holly Jean smiled. Yes, and that one old bachelor was Aunt Kate's former boyfriend, Brother Jake! "Oh, I'm sure someone would buy it, Aunt Kate, seeing it's for a good cause and all. Besides, everyone loves your pies, right?"

"Right! Holly Jean, girl, you talked me into it!"

Just then Granny saw the mail. "Why, child, you didn't tell us we had us some letters! My, my, here's one from my Joe. And from Bea too!"

Peering around for her reading glasses she said, "Now where did those fool specs go to? Guess you'll just have to read them to us yourself, girl."

Holly Jean opened her father's first:

Dear folks:

Hope this finds you three beautiful women just fine. Basic Training is hard, but hard things are necessary in life sometimes. So I do the best I can, knowing that everything they teach me here is something I'm going to need once I get overseas.

Has Mr. Bob started on the new room yet? I sure miss all of you, and Bea too. I gave her our car to take care of while I'm gone. That way she can drive to work instead of taking the bus all the time. She can come down to see you folks too.

Holly Jean, girl, keep practicing your flute. You'll be amazed at the music God can give you even in the darkest hour. I pray for all of you every day.

Please say a good word to the Lord for me too.

Love, Joe

Granny wiped her eyes and blew her nose. "Law, law, so hard to think of him as a grown-up soldier boy. I still see him just a wee shirttail young'un. Well," she cleared her throat, "read us Bea's now, child."

Hi there, Mom, Kate, and Holly Jean!

I hope you're settled in, Holly Jean, and that your new shoes fit. Don't worry about school shoes; I'll get you some in August.

I love my roommates. We're really cramped here, but we have lots of fun together. Susie and JoAnn work with me at the plant. Susie is John's sister and goes with a guy in John's section on the assembly line. We've double-dated for bowling twice. This Saturday we're having a picnic over at Sharon Woods. Then Sunday after church, John's taking me to the movies and roller-skating. I can hardly wait for you to meet him.

I miss you all and hope to see you soon.

All my love, Bea

"Well!" exclaimed Aunt Kate. "Sounds like that young lady's too busy to miss any of us."

Holly Jean was suddenly furious. It wasn't fair! Those were the kind of fun things she'd be getting to do herself if she were back in Cincinnati where she belonged, instead of here in this dump!

But Granny was smiling. "High time that girl got to be around other young folk. She's been an old woman too long."

Instantly, her granddaughter was ashamed. Yes, when she lived with Aunt Bea, her aunt was always too busy working at the factory and at home as well as being Holly Jean's "mother" to get out much. She deserved all the fun in the world.

But Holly Jean deserved some fun too!

Just then Aunt Kate asked, "Why, child, ain't there more writing on the other side?"

Turning the sheet over, Jeannie saw a P.S.

Hey, niece, watch for a package coming next week. I think you'll be very surprised.

    It's something green

      For the keen teen scene.

        Know what I mean?

Not only was Tad Wilson back in church the following Sunday, but he sat right beside Holly Jean. After the service, he pulled out the music to *God Bless America* and grinned.

"All week I've been dying to practice this with you, girl," he said.

But just then Tootsie Anderson and several friends crowded around. Tootsie grabbed his arm. "Tad, darlin', you've just got to meet my sister Annie Sue and my brother Andy. They's both twins, you know. Both sixteen too. Annie Sue plays the saw and Andy does the guitar."

So this was Willie's girl friend! Taller and older than Tootsie, Annie Sue was a very shapely blonde. Big-boned Andy grinned and winked at Holly Jean.

Annie Sue sat on the piano bench by Tad and gave him her brightest smile. "Us eight kids call ourselves the 'Morgan Mills Melody Makers.' We sung twice at camp meeting over to Pine Lick last summer. Folks said we was good enough to be on the radio. Did Tootsie tell you we're gonna sing *This*

World Is Not My Home for the pie social? Well, we're ready to practice with you right now, darlin', if you don't mind."

Miss Linda smiled. "Of course Tad will help, won't you, Tad, dear?"

Tad didn't say yes; he didn't say no. In fact, he didn't say anything at all. Grim-faced, he opened the hymnbook and started playing.

After the group practiced several times, Brother Jake declared, "Well, children, that's mighty good singing. Now we'd all better lock the church up and get on home."

The "Melody Makers" started to leave. Then, as usual, the pastor closed the windows, picked up the trash, and shook hands with Granny and Aunt Kate.

But this time a blushing Aunt Kate didn't let go of his hand.

"Thanks for a fine sermon, Brother Jake," she said. "It really touched me."

Holly Jean was startled. It sure didn't touch *her!*

The old man's face lit up. "W-why, thankee, Miss Kate. Sometimes I pour my heart out and wonder if anyone is even listening. It's hard to do right by God's Word without much book-learning, you know."

"Now, Brother Jake!" Granny protested. "We thank God every day for a faithful preacher like you. Well, we'd better head back up the hollow, Kate, and get the fried chicken on the table."

Aunt Kate fluttered her eyes. "And some of my fine lemon pie."

Brother Jake sighed. "Law, Miss Kate. Lord knows you always made the best lemon pie in the whole county. Ain't had a bite of it in forty years, of course, but a man never forgets good eating like that."

Looking at the two of them, Holly Jean had an idea. "Brother Jake, why don't you come have dinner with us today? I think it's high time you had another piece of Aunt Kate's pie. She still makes them as good as she used to."

He smiled wistfully. "Wouldn't be right to trouble you folks none, Miss Holly Jean."

Tad Wilson had been turning redder and redder. Suddenly, he jumped up from the bench and banged on the piano.

"Wait just a cotton-pickin' minute, Jeannie Roberts!" he shouted. "Why isn't anyone around here worried about troubling *me?* I had to skip my own church service and miss seeing all my other friends to ride all the way out here to these sticks. Then practice some dumb hillbilly song I don't even like with kids who can't even sing! All because I wanted to be with *you!*

"So if you're going off to have fried chicken and pie, when I have to go all the way back to Willow Bend before I get to eat anything, the least you could do is practice with me first!"

His sister paled. "Tad Wilson! Where are your manners?"

Granny snapped her fingers. "Miss Linda, the young man's absolutely right. The Good Book says we're never to let anyone go hungry if we can feed him. And Kate and me can put on the best feed in this whole county.

"So, Brother Jake," Granny grabbed the pastor by the arm, "you just come right along with Kate 'n me and help us put an extra leaf in the kitchen table. When these kids is finished practicing, Miss Linda can lock up and bring them up the hollow. And we'll all have a love feast for the Lord."

"Now, Miz Nanny!" the teacher protested. "You don't have to do this."

Granny laughed. "Lawsy, now, it's our pleasure, isn't it, Kate? Been meaning to have you and Brother Jake over for a coon's age, anyhows."

She put an arm around Tad. "Got chocolate cake too, son, with fudge frosting a whole inch thick and them fancy coconut sprinkles just piled on top. If you're interested that is."

Tad brightened a little. "Well, chocolate *is* my favorite."

"Then it's settled," Granny declared. "Come along, Brother Jake. Time we got those skinny bones of yours fattened up a bit."

After they left, Holly Jean pulled out her flute and opened the music. Inside she was seething at Tad. What a rude, impossible jerk! But when he started playing, she relaxed and let the music soar. He might be a jerk, but he played wonderfully. And he did have great-looking hair.

Afterward, Miss Linda locked the church door, and they drove off in her little coupe down the bumpy road to Granny's.

By the time they reached the cabin, a beaming Brother Jake was more than ready to bless a table piled high with steaming food. Looking around Granny's humble kitchen, Holly Jean was ashamed for these town folk to see how she lived. But they seemed to be having a great time, so she relaxed as well.

"Dear Lord," the pastor prayed, "we thank Thee for the loving hands of the good women as prepared these vittles. May we use its strength to serve Thee. In Jesus' Name. Amen."

Then everyone "set to" eating.

Afterwards, out on the front porch, Tad stretched out his long legs and gave Bear a good petting. "I wish I could have a dog," he confessed. "But I'm allergic to dogs. They give me asthma. I can't have a cat either, but I think they're great. Does your granny have any cats?"

"Oh, yeah. Come and see." Holly Jean and Bear led him out through the meadow of blowing grass and goldenrod to see the wild kittens at the barn. Once there, they sat on hay bales and watched the kittens play around them.

The black and white one she called Domino sniffed Tad's feet and climbed up his pantleg. It even ate a piece of the chicken she dangled to him.

Suddenly—AAACHOOO!

Squealing, the frightened kittens scattered as Tad rummaged frantically through his pockets.

"I've got a handkerchief, if you need one," Holly Jean offered.

His face looked strained. "Thanks, but it's not a cold. It's my allergies bringing on an asthma attack. I mean, with the dog and cats and grass and hay—"

And he had another sneezing fit. "I gotta get out of here."

"Right," Holly Jean agreed. "Back to the house as fast as we can go."

As they hurried back across the field, he sneezed and wheezed more with each painful step.

Then he paused a moment, listening. "Music?" Tad wheezed.

Then she heard it too. The sweet sounds of *In the Garden*. Moon was calling her to the falls.

Beside her, Tad was in serious trouble with his asthma. But if Moon had tried to slip out of the house with his father's picture and his grandfather caught him, his life might be in danger now too.

Dear God! she prayed silently, *which one of them should I try to help first? And what if my help isn't enough for either one?*

Chapter 21
"It's Been Done!"

By now Tad was almost doubled over in his desperate struggle for breath.

"Miss Linda!" Holly Jean screamed. *"HELP!"*

Tad's sister was already flying across the front yard, Brother Jake hard after her. They grabbed the critically ill boy and rushed him inside the cabin.

Granny filled a pan with boiling water from her teakettle and threw in chopped-up pieces of onion. Setting the steaming pan in front of Tad, Granny urged, "Try inhaling the fumes, child. It might help you breathe easier."

Soon Tad stopped his terrible gasping, but he was still pale and weak.

"I'm sorry, Jeannie," he whispered. "I hate this stupid asthma. It makes me feel like a helpless creep. The doctor says I'll outgrow it, but sometimes I don't think I ever will."

Aunt Kate pulled up her rocking chair. "Now you just set thar a spell," she said soothingly. "And don't you worry about a thing, child. Young man can make music like you can's got nothing to be ashamed of, I'd say!"

Miss Linda nodded. "Yes, he should be fine after he rests a bit. I forgot about all the pollen around here. And all those farm animals too!"

At that moment, Holly Jean heard those compelling notes again, fainter but even more urgent: "I come to the garden alone…."

Moon was still calling her. Maybe he had Ben's picture. Maybe he was in danger! But how could she leave Tad, Miss Linda, and Brother Jake?

Then she remembered her plan to ask the teacher to help find Moon's father. Right now was the perfect opportunity to take Miss Linda up to the falls and let her talk to Moon herself!

That is, if she would go.

"Miss Linda," she began, "I know you're dressed for church. But since you and Tad have to stay here awhile anyway, till he feels better, I'd like to show you a waterfall near our house. It's really lovely after all this rain. That is, if you're up to walking."

"A waterfall? I'd love to see it! And don't worry about my high heels, dear. The tires on my car are so old and bald I never know when I'm going to have a flat, so I always keep everyday shoes in the trunk. Give me a minute to change and we're on our way."

As they climbed the steep incline, Holly Jean told Tad's sister all about her mountain's three "ghosts"—the woman who died violently, the woman who floated down from tree-tops, and the "fairy" boy no one else in the world knew about.

"Miss Linda," she concluded, "Moon needs help real

bad. And so do Daisy and her dad. Could you try to help them?"

"Of course, I will! I'd love to have Moon in our school too. What a challenge to teach him to read! But that part about Ben going to work in 'Dubyoupeeay' has me stumped. Never heard of such a place around here. Maybe it's down near Tennessee somewhere. I'll have to look it up in the atlas at the library."

As they neared the falls, Holly Jean's heart began pounding. Would Moon be all right when they got there? What if his mother had caught him with the picture? Or maybe his grandfather….

Then suddenly he was there beside them.

"Oh, Moon, you're all right!" she cried, hugging him. "I'm so glad. Were you able to get your dad's picture?"

"No, Miss Holly Jean, but don't worry. I didn't feel right taking it without Ma's permission, so I asked her about it, and she's bringing it to show you herself. I just hope Grandpa don't find out!" Peering shyly at her guest, Moon asked, "Who's that with you?"

"The teacher I was telling you about, Moon—Miss Linda from Morgan Mills School. She wants to help find your father. Miss Linda, this is Moon."

Just then, Daisy slid down from the tree overhead. Black-eyed Susans garlanded her head, while graceful ferns and Queen Anne's lace trailed down her flowing skirt.

"Howdy there, Ma!" she called. "Sorry you never come by for the cornbread. Pleased to meet you, Miss Teacher-Woman! I used to go to Morgan Mills School too, you know, back when I wasn't no bigger'n a minute. But I like the woods lots better.

"Look all around you, Miss Teacher-Woman—the leaves a-whispering overhead, the birdies all a-flitting and a-singing their little hearts out. God done made 'em all, Miss Teacher-Woman. Ain't never been no book as marvelous as this here forest."

Then she pulled a small picture from her pocket and touched it lovingly. "Moon told me you wanted to see Ben's picture again, Ma. Ah, my sweet, sweet Ben!"

To Miss Linda, Daisy said, "Ben done loved the forest too, Miss Teacher-Woman. Used to log these hills bare till he met me. 'Clearcut,' he called it. I called it 'dirtycut,' 'cause it ain't left nothing behind but sorrow.

"All the little animals with nowhere to go and the dirt just pouring off the hillsides and letting everything go to waste. Well, when I explained that to Ben, he just laid down his ax and never took it up again. It's like killing, it is, Miss Teacher-Woman. Just like killing our land."

Gazing at the towering trees above and around them, Holly Jean was caught in Daisy's spell. Then she remembered her mission.

"Daisy," she began softly, "Miss Linda here wants to look for Ben and bring him back home to you. That's why we need his picture."

Daisy held up a faded snapshot of a handsome young man with night-black hair and sparkling eyes. "Now ain't he the fine-looking one? Remember when I first laid eyes on him, Ma? Him and his brothers was up on this hill logging. And I sees him and I yells, 'No one cuts my trees down, Mister. Now git out of here!' Well, we got to talkin' and he started courtin', and next thing you knows we was gettin' ourselves married.

"He's sure one sweet husband, Ma. Now he's off to Dubyoupeeay to get hisself a job 'cause of the Depression. But he'll be back soon, Ma, you better believe it!"

Miss Linda's eyes glazed with wonder, then filled with tears.

"Of course, Daisy," Holly Jean replied. Fishing for more information, she asked, "And remember where you got married?"

Daisy looked annoyed. "Of course, I remember. I ain't no idiot. You remember too, Ma. Why you ask such silly questions?"

Holly Jean tried again. "Daisy, do you think you could trust Miss Linda and me to borrow your picture for a week or so? When she goes to Dubyoupeeay to find Ben, she'll need it to show folks there what he looks like."

Moon put his arm around his mother. "Please do it, Ma. For me. I want Pa home too."

Daisy held the picture tight against her heart. "It's my onliest picture of him, Miss Teacher-Woman," she quavered. "But I'd rather have my lovin' Ben anytime than just a piece of paper. Please bring it back quick, though, 'causin' I can't rightly sleep without'n it's under my pillow.

"And when you see my Ben, ask him to bring home some white bread and baloney, if it ain't no trouble. A store-boughten broom too, and maybe a mite of cinnamon powder. Oh, and some sunflower seeds. It ain't too late for plantin'.

And some new britches for Moon here. Lawsy, won't Ben be tickled to see how hearty our lad's a-gittin'?"

"Well," Daisy said, suddenly glowing, "I'd better get on back and put a mess of green beans on a-cookin' for him, Miss Teacher-Woman. Oh, he do like my beans. Moon, you want to go pick some dewberries? Your pa always fancied him a good cobbler with plenty of cream."

But Moon grabbed her in sudden terror. "Ma, what'll Grandpa do when Pa comes home? *What if he tries to shoot Pa?*"

Daisy smiled. "Now, chile, you know your grandpa don't mean half what he say. He loves Ben just like we do. We want your pa home, and so does your grandpa. He'll quit his fretting and fussing when Ben's back where he belongs, just you wait and see."

Miss Linda cleared her throat. "I-I'll never let it out of my sight, Daisy, and I'll bring it back as quickly as I can. But it would help if I knew Ben's last name."

Daisy laughed like a tinkly silver bell. "Why, Miss Teacher-Woman, whyn't you just ask Ma? She knows his name gooder'n anyone. It's been done, you know. It's been done."

Suddenly, they heard a man's shout: "Daisy! Moon! Where in tarnation you at?"

Madman Max!

Moon trembled. "You better run, Miss Holly Jean," he whispered, "so Grandpa don't see you. And hide that picture real good!"

Daisy put her arm around him and smiled. "Remember now, Miss Teacher-Woman, not to worry. It's been done."

Then she called, "Coming, Pa!"

Miss Linda stumbled down the hill in a trance. "If I hadn't seen it with my own two eyes, Jeannie," she finally gasped, "I wouldn't have believed it! Well, I believe it now, and I'm going to do something about it! Tomorrow morning I start summer school classes over at Mountain Junction State College. But in the afternoon, I'm going to begin searching through the library, the courthouse, the newspaper office—any place I can think of. Surely someone will recognize this young man and know what's happened to him.

"One thing puzzles me though, Jeannie. Why did Daisy keep saying, 'It's been done'?"

Holly Jean shrugged. "Maybe because she's finally found someone to help her look for her husband."

They could hear Uncle Tom's pickup rattling up to Granny's cabin even before they got there. It was stacked high with boards, nails, tar paper, and metal roof panels.

"Howdy there, Miss Holly Jean!" Uncle Tom boomed. "Howdy, Miss Linda! This lumber's for your new room, gal. Mr. Bob will start on it first thing in the morning. He's bringing young Andy to help him."

Holly Jean smiled. But right then something else caught her attention—the sound of a flute. Her own flute! Tad was on the front porch playing it!

"W-Why, Tad!" she cried. "I had no idea you could play the flute!"

His grin was almost back to normal. "Me neither, so I just tried it out to see. I want to learn all the musical instruments someday, you know. That's why I plan to major in music when I go to college."

His sister gave him a hug. "So glad you're better, dear. Well, time to head on back to Willow Bend, before Mom and Dad wonder what in the world happened to us."

"You can give them a call from up at the store as you pass by, Miss Linda," Uncle Tom replied. "No sense having them all a-worried."

Then the teacher pulled out Ben's picture. "By the way, Granny, Aunt Kate, Pastor Jake, Tom—any of you folks remember seeing this young man?"

Aunt Kate shook her head. "Never forget a face, and I never seed that one before." Neither had the other two.

But Uncle Tom reached out his hand. "Here, let me try. Folks stop by my store from all over, you know. Even Tennessee and West Virginy, sometimes." After studying the snapshot, he said, "Well, feller does bear a resemblance to them four Dunn boys once logged up on Razorback Ridge. From up north, best I remember. I used to stock 'em their supplies. Ain't seen none of them for years, though."

"D-Dunn?" Holly Jean echoed. "You mean the last name might be *Dunn?*"

He nodded. "Doug Dunn's boys. Was in logging till the bottom dropped out of the timber business during the Depression. Why, whatever's the matter, girls?"

For both Holly Jean and Miss Linda thought of the same thing at exactly the same moment. "It's *Ben Dunn!*" they screamed. Grabbing Uncle Tom, they danced the astonished man round and round the yard.

"That's what Daisy was trying to tell us!" Miss Linda cried. "She wasn't saying, 'It's been done.' She was saying, 'It's *Ben Dunn*'!"

Uncle Tom threw his hands up in the air and shook his head in bewilderment.

"Lordy, Lordy!" he sighed. "Guess I never will understand womenfolk as long as I live!"

Chapter 22
Of Corsets and Kitty Cats

The vegetables that Holly Jean, Granny, and Aunt Kate hoed and picked and peeled and sliced and pickled and canned the next week could have fed all the starving people in China.

At least, it seemed that way to a very weary Holly Jean!

All this work was done to the constant pounding of hammers—both Mr. Bob Anderson's and his grandson Andy's. Mr. Bob was kind and jolly. And tall, blond Andy tried to talk with Holly Jean every chance he got.

But whenever she saw him (which was quite often, of course, since they were both working in the very same kitchen), she was reminded of how much she disliked his sister Tootsie, so she could hardly stand to be around him.

Finally, by Friday afternoon, the floor was in, the wall studs up and covered, the rafters in place, a window and siding installed, wallboard hung over the 2x4's, and metal panels nailed onto the rafters for a roof. She had a room of her own.

Then the men patched up the rest of Granny's leaky roof and packed up to leave.

"Don't forget the pie social next week, Red," Andy called

as he climbed into his grandfather's pickup truck. "Bake yourself a pie as good as your Aunt Kate's and I just might bid on it, you lucky girl you."

Don't you dare call me Red! she yelled silently after him. *Only Roger is allowed to call me that!*

The next morning she got out her new birthday stationery and started a letter to Aunt Bea:

Dear Busy Bea:

I adore my birthday presents, and I know I'll love my surprise package too, when it comes. I played a flute solo at church out of the music book you sent. And I'm going to play a duet with Miss Linda's brother at the pie social. She's the teacher here.

My new room is all finished. I wish you were here to share it with me, or that I was there with you. I'm glad you're having such a good time, though. We all want to meet your friend, John. Why don't you bring him to our pie social the Fourth of July if you can get off work? We're going to have music and firecrackers and everything!

I made some new friends here. One of them lives up on Razorback Ridge. His name is Moon. But don't tell Aunt Kate. She thinks there's ghosts up there. I'm helping Moon find his father. I'm also trying to tame the kittens out in the barn. Did you play with the barn cats when you lived here?

Love, Holly Jean

Then to her father:

Hello, Papa Joe!

My new room is beautiful! Miss Linda, the teacher, is giving me some wallpaper for it. And Aunt Kate's going to help me make curtains and an orange-crate desk. I'll be playing my flute at the pie social on the Fourth of July. I wish you were here to hear me and to buy Miss Linda's pie. She's so nice. I hope Brother Jake buys Aunt Kate's. But I don't know who will buy mine. Maybe I'll just eat the whole thing myself!

Hurry and see us as soon as you can. I miss you so much.

Love, Holly Jean

Next came thank-you notes to Roger for the *White Cliffs of Dover* music and his card, and to Shirley, thanking her for her card and picture. Suddenly, she missed them so much she wanted to cry.

Afterward, collecting a shopping list and some letters from Aunt Kate and Granny, she raced Bear down to Morgan Mills to mail everything, and to see if her "surprise package" was in yet.

"Something green for the keen teen scene," her aunt had written. Did that mean green dollar bills? Clothes? Jewelry? Seeds to plant for the garden? Pickles? A green-covered music book?

As she entered, Aunt Tillie called out, "Welcome, welcome, Miss Holly Jean! Got you a package here from your Aunt

Bea. One from Sears for Aunt Kate too. Kate's was a wee bit tore, so I checked it to make sure nothing was damaged. Tell her that's the prettiest corset I ever did see, but she may need a bigger size. And a nice pink-colored one would have been easier to keep clean. What did Bea send you, dear? Package was too taped for me to peek in."

Good for Aunt Bea and that tape! "I don't know, Aunt Tillie. 'Something green,' she said. Can you mail these letters for us?"

"Be proud to, dear. Oh, and here's Kate's new *Sears Fall Catalog.* Can you believe it? Ain't even July, and they's already selling snowsuits and galoshes. Where little Willie is he says it's the same weather all year round—'hot, wet, and lone-some.' Ain't that something? Little Willie was always one to turn a phrase."

Uncle Tom looked up and laughed. "And turn his eyes onto some likely female! You meet that Annie Sue Anderson, Holly? Ain't she a looker? Our little Willie sure can pick 'em!"

Just then the store phone rang—two longs and a short. Uncle Tom picked up the receiver. "Why, she's here right now, Miss Linda. It's for you, Miss Holly Jean."

The party line crackled from static—and from all the people listening in whose numbers *weren't* two longs and a short. "Hello, Jeannie!" the teacher shouted. "Glad I caught you. I was going to leave a message for you. Could you tell Miz Roberts and Sister Kate that we're going to decorate the schoolhouse for the pie social after morning worship tomorrow? That way it'll be ready for Saturday. All you folks listening in on this call are welcome to help too."

After sudden clicks from phones being quickly hung up, Miss Linda said, "By the way, Jeannie, your Aunt Tillie called Dr. Rogers here in town to see if he could come out again to see old Miz Wilma Higgs—that poor lady with tuberculosis who lives up on Sandy Mountain. Tell your aunt that Doc said he'll be out as soon as he gets his car fixed. He broke an axle going up that mountain last time."

But Holly Jean wanted to talk about something entirely different. "Miss Wilson—I mean, Miss Linda! Did you find out anything about our—uh, 'business'?"

There was silence at the other end. Then, "Y-Yes, dear. B-But the news isn't good. We'll talk more about it tomorrow."

On the way back up the hollow, Holly Jean's arms were full of groceries, plus both packages—hers and Aunt Kate's. But her heart was even heavier. Miss Linda said the news wasn't good. Did that mean Ben Dunn had disappeared from Dubyoupeeay also? Or died? Or committed some horrible crime? Or even that Madman Max had already found him and killed him?

Poor Daisy was already almost crazy with grief. How would she act if they had to tell her she would never see her Ben again? And what would happen to poor Moon?

As she neared Granny's cabin, only half aware of her surroundings, Holly Jean suddenly noticed a little black and white kitten at her feet, right there in the middle of the road.

Even stranger, Bear wasn't sniffing it and wagging his tail. With a wild yelp, he took off as fast as he could.

Well, obviously this lost kitten belonged back in the barn. Setting her packages down, she reached out both arms. "Time to go home now, Kitty!" she cooed.

But just as she picked it up, she realized something else: This was not a little black and white barn kitten. In fact, this kitten belonged to another species of animal entirely.

Skunk!

And it was aiming its tail straight at her!

Holly Jean was so astonished, she couldn't even scream.

Never in her life had she encountered an odor so absolutely foul. Worse, this one wasn't drifting in on the breeze from far, far away.

She smelled it on *herself!*

The cute little creature she had tried to help had simply turned tail on her and sauntered off, head in the air. But not before leaving his calling card all over Holly Jean—and her packages, as well! Bear, though, escaped—hightailing it for home the moment he spotted danger.

Granny and Aunt Kate could smell Holly Jean's "present" all the way back at the cabin. And when she dragged herself, bawling, into the front yard, they went into action. Holding tightly to their noses, they grabbed her and hauled her to the backyard. There, clothes and all, she was dumped into soapy, scalding water in Granny's big washtub. Over and over again.

Each time Granny and Aunt Kate poured the putrid water out onto the garden, they filled the tub right back up and pushed her in again. When all the hot water on the stove was gone, they drew some fresh from the well—freezing cold.

The packages she'd been carrying had been drenched, too. Of the groceries, only the canned goods could be saved, while the packages from Sears and Aunt Bea went right into the tub as well.

"My brand-new corset!" Aunt Kate wailed. "My extra-support special with whalebones and lace and ties and all those pretty unmentionables! First new one I've had in twenty-five years, and it ain't even been worn. What if it shrinks?"

But it didn't. And neither did Aunt Bea's "green surprise"—a kelly green peasant jumper with full skirt and sweetheart neckline, with embroidery all over in delicate pink and white roses and deep green leaves. Her aunt must have spent hours sewing it!

Washed and starched and flapping in the breeze on Granny's clothesline, her new jumper looked absolutely beautiful. So did its matching white peasant blouse, with ruffled elastic neck and short, puffy sleeves. Just perfect for the pie social!

But no amount of washing, even in Granny's strong lye soap, could save Holly Jean's old gym shoes. With a clothespin firmly on her nose, Granny finally buried them in the potato patch.

Holly Jean had already lost her school shoes. She could wear her new dress-up sandals to the pie social. But now what would she wear to go to the store or around the farm? Even up to the falls?

When at last Granny brought her inside, she was shaking so badly her teeth rattled. Granny wrapped her up in a flannel nightgown and thick socks, covered her with a quilt, and set her at the kitchen table with a hot cup of soup.

"Poor child," sighed her grandmother. "Just hope you don't come down with a cold now."

Before long, Holly Jean was sneezing, coughing, and blowing her nose uncontrollably. Now she understood why Tad hated his asthma so much. Being sick was the pits!

Granny brought Holly Jean's mattress, quilts, and clothes down from the attic, and that night she slept in her new room for the very first time. Granny even let Bear sleep with her to keep her warm.

By next morning, her cold was much better, and she looked forward to going to church, all "dolled" up in her best yellow dress and white sandals.

But the real "glamour girl" that day was Aunt Kate! Granny had tugged and pulled and pushed her sister's generous body into her new corset, then laced and tied it as tightly as possible. Over her new figure, Aunt Kate wore a pretty, pink-print, flour-sack dress, instead of her usual dark gray one. She had even sat up late the night before and sewed flirty lace ruffles all around the edge of her best poke-bonnet.

Last of all, Aunt Kate heated a curling iron on the kitchen stove to coax a few silver ringlets around her face. Then she dabbed rouge on her plump cheeks.

Holly Jean danced around her. "Aunt Kate! You look positively gorgeous! Why, Brother Jake will have to be blind not to go gaga over you! And not just over your pies!"

The church house was fuller than ever that morning. Tad wasn't there, but Andy played his guitar along with the singing—and was surprisingly good. If only he'd quit winking at all the girls, as if he had dust in his eye or something!

Besides, she had another boy on her mind today, Moon Dunn, and his father, Ben.

During announcement time, Miss Linda invited everyone to stop by the schoolhouse next door after services to help decorate it for Saturday.

Next, Aunt Tillie asked prayer for poor old Miz Wilma Hogg. "Me 'n Brother Jake gonna take Doc Rogers up to see her this week and fetch along some vittles. She's really ailing now with her consumption. Doc says he may have to drive her to Lexington to the TB hospital. And y'all know what a homebody that poor old soul is."

Then Aunt Kate stood up in all her finery. Holding their one hymnbook aloft, she said, "We had great singing this morning, didn't we, folks? But it would be even better if we all had hymnbooks to sing from like we used to, years ago. Well, if we can raise enough money next Saturday night, we'll buy fifty of them! And a new heatin' stove for the schoolhouse. And if they's any money left over, why, we'll fix up the old pianer too!

"Last time this church bought hymnbooks, more'n twenty years ago, they was only twenty cents apiece. Now they's up to a dollar. That's $50.00 right there, plus another $50.00 for the stove. Plus more for the pianer. And all the money in our treasury right now is $2.87."

Aunt Tillie raised her hand. "If we can raise $100.00 for the stove and books, Sister Kate, Tom 'n me'll pay for the piano tunin' in our little Willie's name. Lord, how much that poor boy loves him a good Gospel singin'."

Aunt Kate beamed. "Praise the Lord, Sister Tillie. Remember, it's all for a good cause. We'll have lots of special music. Brother Jake will give us a word from the Bible. And there'll be a cakewalk and contests and homemade ice cream. Firecrackers, too. And plenty of pretty girls—I mean pies—for you young blades to bid over!"

Everyone laughed, as she quite meant for them to.

"Fact is, I'll be bringing one of my famous lemon pies myself! So start saving up your nickels, dimes, and quarters, fellers!" And she smiled right at Brother Jake as she sat down.

Holly Jean smiled too. *Way to go, Aunt Kate!*

"Amen, amen!" exclaimed the pastor. "Well, it's good to see so many of you in the house of the Lord this morning! Keep up this attendance, and we'll be able to start up Sunday school again! Sister Kate, remember when we had us a hundred or more here every single Sunday? And remember…."

Suddenly, he stopped, turning pale. And very sad. Then he went directly into his sermon.

Holly Jean wondered what it was he remembered. Did it have anything to do with her great-aunt?

Over at the schoolhouse afterward, everyone went into action. Using their construction ladders, Andy and his grandfather strung crepe paper streamers across the ceiling and down the dangling bare lightbulb wires. The other men moved the desks into a circle around the wall. The women washed the desks and the floor, while the children cleaned the blackboards and windows. That is, when they weren't outside playing tag.

"Only been a month since classes was out," Granny complained. "How in tarnation this place get so dirty with no one here?"

Then the state and national flags were installed in their brackets. Miss Linda smiled at it all approvingly.

"It's a shame rubber's so hard to get these days," she said. "Balloons would be the crowning touch! But maybe some of you can bring some red, white, and blue flowers so everything will look patriotic."

Finally, the workers streamed out into the schoolyard to head for home—proud, tired, and ready for Sunday dinner. Andy caught up with Holly Jean on the steps and grabbed her hand.

"Hey, Red," he teased, "you keep snubbing me like this and I'll buy your pie just in spite. Won't be able to ignore me then, will you?"

She pulled her hand free and grinned back. "Only kind of pie you deserve, Andy Anderson, is 'humble pie'! Bet you never had any of that in your entire life!"

He laughed. "Okay, Smart Mouth, we'll see what happens come Saturday. Just make sure your pie has a flaky crust. Can't stand a soggy one. And remember, with hair that red, no way you can hide from me no matter how big the crowd is."

"Huh! You've got enough crust yourself for *two* pies, Andy," she retorted, enjoying the teasing.

Until she caught Tootsie glaring at her. "Fatty, fatty, Cincinnati Catty," Tootsie muttered. "Don't worry, little darlin', I'm going to make sure nobody buys your pie! *Nobody!*"

As people drifted away, Holly Jean and Miss Linda walked back through the cemetery to the teacher's car. "Miss Linda!" she finally burst out. "I can't stand the suspense another minute! Please—what happened to Moon's father?"

The teacher put her arm around Holly Jean's shoulders. "Well, dear, the first part's almost funny in a sad sort of way. You see, during the Depression many people, like Moon's father, were out of work and couldn't find jobs to feed their families. So the Government set up a way to help poor people and the entire nation at the same time—by paying them to work. Building roads, bridges, schoolhouses, dams, that sort of thing.

"Jeannie, Moon's father didn't leave home to go to work in a town called 'Dubyoupeeay.' There's no such place! No, he was headed for Mountain Junction to sign up for the Works Progress Administration. Better known as the *W.P.A.!*"

Dubyoupeeay? W.P.A.?

When Holly Jean thought that one through, she was convulsed with giggles. "Why, Miss Linda, that's as ridiculous as 'Ben Dunn/been done'! Can't Daisy ever get anything right? Then what?"

The teacher sighed. "Well, about the same time that Ben Dunn apparently disappeared, a bus full of W.P.A. recruits left from Mountain Junction for Lexington. But the bus didn't make it. Sliding off a mountain road in a torrential rainstorm, it crashed and burned, leaving only a few survivors.

"I found some newspaper accounts of the accident down at the library. Pete Curtiss—he's editor of *The Willow Bend Weekly*—helped me too. According to the writeups, a young man answering Ben Dunn's description was a real hero. Single-handedly pulled several people from the flaming bus.

"It was hard to get a list of either the dead or the survivors, though. None of the bus passengers had signed up yet on the W.P.A. register. And many of the dead were burned beyond recognition. The critically injured were taken on to Lexington, but no one was admitted to any of the hospitals there under Ben's name.

"However, someone did find this little snapshot laying near the scene of the accident and put it in the Lexington newspaper."

And she held out a clipping. *It was a picture of Daisy!*

Soberly, Miss Linda continued, "Jeannie, this would explain why no one ever contacted Daisy or Mr. Morgan—or even Ben's own parents—about the accident. No one knew he was involved."

Holly Jean broke into sobs. "Oh, Miss Linda, it's just not fair! Daisy and Moon love him so much. He's got to be alive somewhere! He's just got to!"

Miss Linda wiped her eyes. "That's what I'm hoping and praying for too, Jeannie. That's why I told my classmates at college about it this week. The professor's sending a copy of Ben's picture to the Mountain Junction paper and to the Lexington paper. And Pete's putting it in the Willow Bend paper, and in as many more around the state as possible. If Ben Dunn can be found alive, we'll find him."

Just then Holly Jean trembled. Crossing the cemetery, they had reached a sadly familiar grave covered with faded lilacs. Mama Jean's. Yes, her own mother had died suddenly in a terrible accident years ago. Is that what had happened to Moon's father too?

If so, where was his grave?

And how could they ever tell Daisy?

Before Miss Linda drove off, Holly Jean handed her the precious five-dollar bill given her by Papa Joe. Then she explained about the skunk.

"So now I don't have any everyday shoes to wear around here, Miss Linda, or to hike in up to the falls. Uncle Tom doesn't carry shoes in his store, so I wondered if you could buy me some gym shoes in town since you don't need ration stamps to buy them. Nothing fancy. I hope this is enough money."

"No trouble at all, dear. There're shoe stores in both Willow Bend and Mountain Junction. I'll try to pick up a pair this week and bring them to the pie social. By the way, Tad said to tell you he intends to buy your pie!"

On their walk back up their hollow, Aunt Kate fairly floated above the bumpy road, her lame knee and cane quite forgotten.

"Oh, Nan!" she cried. "If only Brother Jake buys my pie this time—to help make up for all those years I done been all tore up inside with hurt. If only it's not too late to get things right! If only we're not too old to start over!"

Granny patted her arm. "Now, it's never too late to right a wrong, Kate. And we're never too old to seek and to give happiness. Remember Great-great-grandpa Ebenezer? Widower for thirty years he was; then married again at eighty-five. Danced at his own wedding too!"

Her granddaughter was intrigued. "Right what 'wrong,' Granny?"

The two women looked at each other. "Never mind, Holly Jean," her grandmother answered sharply. "You're too young to understand."

But she wasn't! She'd already had a lifetime of heartbreak, what with losing her poor Mama Jean. So had Moon with his father. *Please, God, help someone find out something good about Ben Dunn this week. Please don't let him be dead!*

Granny changed the subject. "Holly Jean, how about you 'n me going berrypickin' this week and making some nice preserves? You can take some pie-making lessons from your Aunt Kate too. You'll want the yummiest pie possible for Saturday, and the fetchingest box in the whole schoolhouse!"

"Box? You mean, the pies are sold in boxes where no one can even see them?"

Aunt Kate laughed. "Fellers can see what's inside after they buy them, of course, but not a minute before. Fact is, they've got to take someone's word for it that there's really anything inside! If a feller likes the girl enough, he don't really care what's in the box. He just wants to sit and look into her eyes and talk and maybe hold her hand. 'Course, if the pie's yummy, that's even better!"

Granny swooped down and picked a dandelion. Then she held it teasingly under Holly Jean's chin. "Ah, ha! Yellow face! Shows you like butter!"

More seriously, she said, "Sometimes, Holly Jean, two or three fellers aim to buy the same girl's box. Then things can get a mite testy. Usually bidding on the pies starts about ten cents or a quarter. But when there's fierce competing, it can go high as five dollars. Even ten!"

Aunt Kate touched the new lace on her bonnet dreamily. "But it's all for a good cause. The more people pay, the more money we'll have for our new hymnbooks and school stove."

What if both Tad and Andy bid on Holly Jean's pie, as they promised to do? Would things get a "mite testy" then? Or would Tootsie somehow make good on her threat to make sure *no one* bought it?

She drifted off to sleep that night thinking of nothing but the big Fourth of July pie social. But when she awoke in the middle of the night, gasping for breath and drenched with sweat, all she could think of was "*Granny!*"

Nan Roberts rushed in with a hastily lit kerosene lamp. "Why, you poor child!" she cried. "You did take cold, after all!

"Here, Kate," Granny roused her sister from a sound sleep, "get out the mustard and camphor, and some flannel rags. She needs cough syrup, and aspirin for that fever. Holly Jean, love, open up your mouth. I have some nice lemon and honey for you. Kate, get the teakettle a-boiling! Sounds like she's going into croup!"

For the next couple of days Holly Jean drifted in and out of feverish dreams as Granny and Aunt Kate bustled around her. Bear whined pitifully outside, longing to be by her side.

When she finally started feeling better, Granny let her sit on a rocking chair out on the front porch with Bear, to enjoy the afternoon breeze.

And that's when she heard it, wafting gently but unmistakably down the mountain: "And the joy we share as we tarry there, none other has ever known."

In the Garden. Moon was calling her back to the falls.

Please, dear God, help Moon with whatever problem he's having right now. And help me get well for Saturday. As soon I get my new gym shoes, I'll go see him. Maybe by then we'll have news about his father.

Since Holly Jean was still too weak to make her usual weekly trip down to the store, Aunt Kate volunteered to go. In fact, Granny couldn't keep her home! And when she returned, she was not only *not* using her cane—she hopped right up the porch steps two at a time!

"It come, Nan!" she cried exultantly. "It come! I'm so flibbertigibbeted I can hardly stand it." Granny rushed out in alarm. "Sit down, woman, afore you fall down! What come?"

"My Sears order, that's what!"

"Well, I knowed that. You got it last week."

"No, no—this is another one! Oh, law, Nan, you know I ain't had any storeboughten clothes for years and years! It's all been flour-sack and make-do and hand-me-downs. Until today!"

Tearing open her package, she cried, "Look, Nan! New shoes! You ever seen such pure white laces? And feast your eyes on this stylish frock! With its own belt, and buttons a-gleamin' like genuine pearls! Why, I feel as proud as a hen showing off her chicks. I've got to go right inside and try it all on this very minute!"

After plopping her treasures down on her bed, Aunt Kate stood in the middle of the sitting room, while Granny and Holly Jean helped her on with her new blue dress and white oxfords. Touching the delicate lace collar, the tiny buttons, the front tucks and large sheer sleeves, Aunt Kate's eyes were bright with wonder.

"Ain't never wore nothing so plumb pretty in all my born days!" she bubbled, eyes bright with tears. "Nan, this-here is what I aims to sashay in down to that pie social. Won't I be a stunner!"

And then she looked down at her legs.

"Lord have mercy!" she shrieked. "They've cheated me, Nan! Plumb cheated me! Done cut the whole bottom of my skirt right off!"

Holly Jean giggled. "No one cheated you, Aunt Kate. Remember when Aunt Bea told you that women's skirts are shorter now? Using less fabric helps us fight the war."

Her great-aunt still stared down, bug-eyed. Then she twirled around, turning this way and that, watching herself in the old dresser mirror. Finally, she announced, "Well, John Higgs always did say I had good legs."

She looked sternly at Granny. "All right, Nan, done made up my mind. Now, you know, I'm a good Christian woman, and I'd never dream of sewing me a dress this scandalous. But if wearing it helps bring poor Joe and Willie home, why— why, I'll do it! Let all the tongues wag as wants to!"

And she whirled dreamily all around the room like a ballerina on some faraway stage.

Chapter 25
The Big Pie Social

By Saturday morning Holly Jean was almost well again. After a good hot bath in the washtub by the kitchen stove, she helped Granny and Aunt Kate prepare for the big night ahead.

Already the kitchen was filled with the scrumptious aromas of pies—lemon, rhubarb, blackberry, chocolate, custard, butterscotch, and mince. Even with sugar rationing, honey and molasses produced right in Morgan Mills made them all deliciously sweet. Three of the pies would be boxed up for special bidding, while the rest could be purchased by any of the partygoers.

"How are we going to get them all down to the schoolhouse?" she wondered.

"Tom's going to take us, child," Aunt Kate replied. "Don't think I'm going to get my new shoes ruined afore I've even showed them off, do you?"

Later that afternoon, Holly Jean worked on her pie container. Her blackberry pie fit perfectly inside Aunt Kate's Sears box. And the gold paper and silver ribbon from Aunt Bea's birthday present were just the right size to wrap it up with.

Then just as she tied the final bow, she heard it again: "And He walks with me, and He talks with me…."

Moon!

Moon, don't you understand? I can't come now. Wait till I go to the pie social and find out more about your pa and get my new gym shoes to hike in. Then I'll be up there to see you, I promise.

Oh, if only their families had telephones like "civilized" people!

By the time Uncle Tom's truck rumbled up the road, Holly Jean was almost too excited to stand still. Her new peasant outfit fit her perfectly, while the beautiful stone necklace Aunt Kate had given her sparkled like a ruby.

"Gal," Granny exclaimed, "with your red hair and that green dress, the fellers' eyes are going to pop! And, Kate, you're a knockout too!"

Her sister twirled about again in her new dress. "Maybelle Morgan liked to wear green with her red hair, Holly. Max always said it was her bestest color." Stopping for a moment, she went on, "Nan, think I should take off my shoes and put on some new corn plasters afore we go?"

Uncle Tom jumped out of the truck cab, whistling. "Lawsy, look at that! The three best-looking gals in the entire county!"

Then they all climbed into the truck. Aunt Kate and Jeannie sat in the truck bed on crates, with all the extra pies. Granny sat in front with Uncle Tom and the pie boxes: her own red one, a blue one for Aunt Kate, and the gold one for Holly Jean.

As they bounced along, Holly Jean held tightly to her flute case. "Aunt Kate, everyone says Brother Jake is very poor.

Maybe he won't have enough money to buy your pie tonight. Couldn't you still like him anyway?"

Her great-aunt's face turned dark. "That cheapskate! He better not try that again! I've still never forgiven him!"

Then her jaw dropped and her lip trembled. "Oh, Holly Jean, I can't believe I said that! Of course, I like him. I'll love him till the day I die. But, see, it can't be just one way. He's got to show he likes me too. It can't be that hard, can it? I mean, it's just one little blue pie box. Am I too old to have a little happiness in life?"

"Of course not, Aunt Kate. You look absolutely beautiful this evening. No way Brother Jake can keep his eyes off you!" *Please, God, make that come true.*

They could hear shouts, laughter, and firecrackers long before they reached the schoolhouse.

"Lawsy, ain't this some turnout?" cried a delighted Aunt Kate.

Pulling up in front of his store, Uncle Tom helped the women dismount from the truck and carry their pies across the road to the schoolhouse. Then he hurried back to his store to help all the waiting customers. No pie social for him; with this many people come to "town," he'd be busy at his store all night.

Andy was out in front of the schoolhouse with some friends. "Aha, Red Roberts!" he exclaimed when he saw her. "I see you brought yourself a fancy gold-spangled box to try to catch my eye with. But I ain't bidding on it less'n the pie crust is flaky the way I like it." And he gave her a big wink.

Laughing, Aunt Kate answered for her. "Why, son, that pie's so light, Holly Jean has to hold onto it with both hands to keep it from floating plumb away!"

Miss Linda's big desk at the front of the room and the small desks around it were piled high with pie boxes. Cookies and cakes of every description, and shiny jars of jellies and jams were tucked in for good measure. Nearby were three hand-cranked tubs of homemade ice cream.

Aunt Tillie and some of the other women were checking the pie boxes in. Tootsie was helping too.

Aunt Tillie clapped with delight when she saw Holly Jean's box. "Will you look at that, Miss Tootsie! Shiny as a sunrise, it is! Oh, Miss Holly Jean, dear, will you tell your Aunt Kate that Brother Jake 'n me went up to poor old Miz Wilma's with Doc today? Doc said it'd cost a hundred bucks to put her in the TB hospital, so Jake paid him and Doc took off with her. It's all for the best, you know. Poor woman; she was a-suffering so."

Tootsie waited till Aunt Tillie turned away. Then she smiled at Holly Jean, but not a kind smile. "Yes, it *is* a highfalutin' box, Miss Cincinnati Catty. Shame no one's ever going to see what's in it!"

A voice inside Holly Jean yelled: *Don't leave the pie! She's going to do something to it!*

But just then Tad grabbed her arm and pulled her over to the piano. "Thought you'd never get here!" he fussed. "Don't you know the program's starting in five minutes? Sis wants to begin with the Pledge of Allegiance and *The Star-Spangled Banner*. Then it's our *God Bless America* duet. Pete

Curtiss here—Sis' friend from the newspaper—is helping out on drums."

Mr. Curtiss had already set up his instruments. Quiet looking, bespectacled, and balding, he had a warm smile and even warmer handshake. "Welcome to Kentucky, Jeannie. Linda's told me a lot about you, and about your friend, Mr. Dunn too. I've asked newspapers all over the state to print his picture this week. Surely someone will recognize him."

Miss Linda hurried over. "Don't forget to take plenty of pictures tonight, Pete. I want the whole county to know that we're putting Morgan Mills back on the map."

Then she handed Holly Jean back her still-crisp five-dollar bill. "Got your new gym shoes out in the car," she said, "but I didn't have to pay a cent for them. The shoe store in Mountain Junction had a pair just your size that someone returned. The owner there's an old friend of mine. Said since these have a dirty splotch on one side and no box to put them in, you can have them for free. I explained you just wanted something to hike around in, anyway."

Holly Jean thanked her, tucked the money into her jumper pocket, and unpacked her flute. Then someone rang the school bell, and the people outside started pouring in for the evening's program.

After the Pledge and the National Anthem came *God Bless America* and a moment of silent prayer for the servicemen and women overseas. Then the rest of the "special music" began.

The "Morgan Mills Melody Makers" sang three songs, not just one, and they were much better than Holly Jean expected. With Tad at the piano, Andy on the guitar, Annie Sue on the musical saw, Mr. Curtiss on the drums, and Jeannie on the flute, the audience was soon on their feet, clapping joyfully along.

Next came the Men's Quartet and several duets. Old Mr. Allerbee from Pine Lick did some foot-stomping numbers on his fiddle, while his cousin played the banjo. Then Aunt Kate and Granny sang a duet of *Amazing Grace*, with everyone joining in.

Everyone, that is, but Brother Jake. Holly Jean hadn't seen him all evening. Where in the world was he?

By now the sky outside was as black as Tad's hair. Looking out the schoolhouse window, she saw a full moon just beginning to rise behind the darkened church.

And something else.

Two pale forms hovered among the tombstones out in the graveyard, singing right along with everyone else.

Daisy and Moon.

Holly Jean was so startled she almost dropped her flute. All week long Moon had been trying to reach her. Now he and his mother had come all the way down to Morgan Mills to find her—Daisy here for the first time since her mother's funeral years ago; Moon for the first time in his entire life! If they were that willing to brave Max Morgan's fury to tell her something, it must really be important!

Nudging Tad, Holly Jean said, "Look, I've got to go outside. Right now."

"Not by yourself," he whispered back. "It's too dark. Wait till this song's over and I'll go with you."

Finally, the music stopped and Andy's grandfather announced the cakewalk. As the laughing contestants headed for the chalked lines on the schoolroom floor Tad and Holly Jean slipped out the door.

She strained to see across the night-black cemetery. Maybelle Morgan's tall, white tombstone was lit eerily by the rising moon. Daisy and Moon were right beside it! Her friends couldn't have looked more like ghosts if they had tried.

Tad grabbed her arm. "W-Who's that?"

"Shhh! The people your sister's trying to help. They want to tell me something. That's why I came outside."

Just then the door of the church next door flew open. Out ran a man, sobbing as if his heart would break. Stumbling across the cemetery, he fell to the ground in front of Maybelle Morgan's tombstone. Daisy and Moon slipped back into the shadows.

Now Holly Jean could see the man's face in the moonlight. It was Brother Jake!

"Dear Lord, forgive me!" he cried out. "And forgive my poor brother too. He kilt poor Maybelle here, but I done something just as bad. I done broke my poor, sweet Kate's heart and let it stay broke these forty years now!

"Oh, if only I'd had the money to buy her pie back then! If only Pa 'n me hadn't had that falling out, so's I lost everything! But, dear Lord, you know that for two years now I've been saving up every penny I could get so's I could make it right with my little Katie and ask her to be my sweet bride. Got all of one hundred dollars together, I did! More'n enough to rent us a nice little place somewhere. And then poor Miz Wilma had to go to the hospital and...."

He shook with sobs. "Here I was planning to bid five whole dollars on my sweet girl's pie tonight to show her how much I prize her. And n-now I can't bid n-nothing at all. Her poor heart gonna be broke all over again!"

Tears rolled down Holly Jean's cheeks. Brother Jake was suffering just because he was so kind, and now he needed five dollars and didn't have it.

But she did!

Please, dear God, she prayed. *Let this help him.*

Snatching the five-dollar bill from her jumper pocket, she crept from tombstone to tombstone until she reached Maybelle Morgan's grave. Laying the money in front of the still-praying preacher, she slipped back to Tad.

Soon Brother Jake lifted up his eyes and saw the five-dollar bill there in the moonlight.

"A-a *miracle*!" he whispered. "Oh, dear Heavenly Father, I don't know how You done that. But I do know You're in the miracle business, and this sure seems a miracle to me! Oh, Lordy, Lordy! Hallelujah!"

And, still waving the five-dollar bill, he ran straight across the cemetery, up the steps two at a time, and right into the schoolhouse.

Wiping the tears from her eyes, Holly Jean turned around to talk with Daisy and Moon, but they had vanished as well!

Tad shivered. "I don't understand this, Jeannie. I don't understand any of this! And I'm not sure I want to. It's all too creepy for me. Let's go on back inside before someone misses us."

But someone already had. Striding across the graveyard toward them came a very angry Andy. Grabbing Tad's arm, he roared, "Hey, City Slicker! What in tarnation you doing out here in the dark with Red?"

Oh, no, dear God! Don't let them fight!

"Goodness, Andy," she replied. "Cool it, will you? We had to get Brother Jake for the pie auction. He didn't want to miss out bidding on Aunt Kate's pie. Didn't he pass you just now?"

Well, at least part of what she said was true.

Still scowling, Andy looked closely at both of them, then let Tad go. "Huh! Listen, Red, next time you want to go somewhere, you ask *me* to go with you, you hear?"

As they walked in, Aunt Tillie was just finishing announcing that the ice cream was now frozen and ready for sale. Then it was time for the pie auction.

Mr. Bob was the auctioneer. "Well, well," he boomed, "whose box should we start with tonight?"

"The beautiful blue one!" shouted a familiar voice. "Start with Sister Kate's!"

Everyone stared, then gasped. *Brother Jake*! But how strange he looked—with his clothes all messed up, grass stains on his knees, and a five-dollar bill waving in his hand!

"If I didn't know better," sniffed Aunt Tillie, "I'd say the poor man was drunk!"

Mr. Bob laughed. "Well, all right then. The pastor wants us to start with Sister Kate's box." Holding it aloft, he said, "Now you fellers know that Kate Barkley bakes the finest pies in this here county. So who wants to start the bidding on this pretty blue box—as blue as the dress Sister Kate's wearing tonight? Do I hear a quarter?"

"Five dollars!" Brother Jake shouted.

Titters rippled across the room. "Well, now, Brother Jake," the auctioneer replied gently, "you don't have to start that high. Let's get a little competition going. Do I hear fifty cents?"

But the minister ran to the front of the room. "No! *Five dollars—and not a penny less!*"

Tears shone in his eyes. "'Cause all the gold in Ft. Knox wouldn't be as wonderful as eating that pie with the sweetest woman in the world." And he stared straight at a blushing Aunt Kate.

Gasps from the crowd—then cheers!

"Tell you what," chuckled the auctioneer. "I'm just a-going to declare bidding on this here box officially closed. Sold to Jake Morgan—for the princely sum of five whole dollars!"

The pastor looked ten feet tall as he walked over to claim his prize.

Mr. Curtiss took a flash picture, and the room resounded with applause.

"Keep up that bidding, folks," Mr. Bob remarked, "and we'll have our stove and hymnbooks paid for in no time. All right, whose box is next?"

Tootsie's was, then Annie Sue's, and on and on, with bidding brisk and lively. Pete Curtiss bought Miss Wilson's. Mr. Allerbee, the fiddler, won Granny's, and his six-year-old grandson got Aunt Tillie's. In no time, twenty-three boxes had been sold.

The suspense of waiting for her own name to be called became almost more than Holly Jean could bear. Who would bid on her pie? And who would end up getting it?

"Well, folks," concluded the auctioneer, "that's the last of the pie boxes. But if you missed out, you can still buy some of these other delicious goodies up here. Sister Tillie and Miss Linda, could you two total up our receipts so far, then report back to us in a bit?

"All right, next up is our egg-and-spoon contest—just for the kids!"

Holly Jean's box hadn't been called at all!

Andy waved his arms. "Hey, Grandpa! What about Red Roberts' box?"

"Yeah!" echoed Tad. "It was the gold one—right in the middle."

Aunt Tillie fluttered her arms. "Land o' Goshen, Holly Jean! I checked it in myself, I did! Sparkly ribbon and everything! It was number seventeen."

Mr. Bob put a comforting arm around Holly Jean's shoulders. "Well, now, ain't that most peculiar? But don't you fret, young lady. We'll find your pie for you. It's got to be around here somewhere."

She seemed to see and hear everything from far, far away. No, no, this couldn't possibly be happening! Then she saw Tootsie's gleeful grin. *Oh, yes,* it seemed to say, *it could.*

And it did!

Chapter 27
Brother Jake's Confession

Tad took her hand. "Don't cry, Jeannie. Look, I'll just buy one of the extra pies, and we can eat that, okay?"

Andy patted her other hand. "I'm sorry, Red, really I am. Hey, I'll buy one of those other pies too, and we'll all three eat together, if that's all right by Tad. But I tell you one thing: if I ever find the skunk who pulled this dirty trick…." He pounded one fist into the other.

More contests followed, including a lemonade chug-a-lug and a husband-calling contest. Then Aunt Tillie and Miss Linda gave their financial report.

"We're up to $87.28 so far!" exclaimed the teacher. "And we've still got the rest of the unboxed pies and cakes and ice cream for sale!"

To loud cheers, Mr. Bob added, "And now, before we eat, Brother Jake has a word for us from the Good Book."

The stooped minister stood up, his worn Bible in one hand, Aunt Kate's blue pie box in the other.

"Folks," he began quietly, "I was asked to give you a little sermon tonight. Well, instead, I'm going to tell you a little story. Only it's not little to me. It's the story of my life.

"Tonight the good Lord helped me buy this pie. And I'm mighty gratified, but not just 'cause that lady's the best pie-baker in the county. Why, I wouldn't care if this box was teetotally empty, 'cause I'd gladly pay every cent I own just to tell Kate and the rest of you good people here tonight how I feel about her. I'm just sorry I couldn't do that at the last pie social I went to here, over forty years ago."

Holly Jean sat on the edge of her seat, her own pie box troubles quite forgotten. People usually slept when Brother Jake preached. Tonight they were all wide awake!

At fourteen, Jake Morgan explained, he had received Christ as his personal Savior, "over at Pine Lick Camp Meeting." At sixteen, he felt called to preach.

"Pa humored me for a while. He thought I'd outgrow it. Besides, he was glad to have me 'n Max out with nice girls and not carousing around. Ma, bless her heart, rejoiced every day, but Pa didn't take no truck with churchified things hisself. Figured real men should tend to business and make lots of money for their families like he did.

"Well, Pa knew Max was serious about Maybelle, and me about Kate. Pa was always partial to Sister Kate, you know. Called her 'Jake's Cutie-Pie.' Said she deserved the best money could buy, and Kate quite agreed with him."

Aunt Kate turned red, but she nodded.

"Hershell Morgan had his mills and them two big farms. My brother Max helped out with the Razorback Ridge property, and I was in charge of the bottomland one. Pa'd lend us money during the year. Then, end of season when the crops and livestock sold, we'd pay him back. He said we could have the farms fair and square what time we was ready to marry and be on our own.

"But what God really called me to was preaching His Word. I wanted some book-learnin' to help me do it right. So I asked Pa if I worked summers on the farm, could I go to Bible school down Simpsonville way during the winters. This was the day before pie social time, forty years ago."

Angry, his father not only refused to allow Jake to go to school, but announced he would never lend or give him "one red cent" from that day forward—not even the money Jake had already earned. Nor would he let him borrow the family horses or carriage. From then on, Jake would be completely on his own—at least until he "came to his senses."

"Poor Kate!" he continued, wiping his eyes. "Everyone knowed we was sweet on each other. What they didn't know was that I was now stone-broke. So when I didn't take her to the social—and didn't bid as much as a penny on her pie, but let John Higgs buy it—well, my little Kate thought I was shaming her for sure."

Aunt Kate jumped up, sobbing. "I-I certainly did, Jake Morgan! Been grieving over that for forty year now! Whyn't you say something, Jake? Whyn't you let me know?"

He gave a sad smile. "Well, now, Kate, sweet, I sure tried to, I did. But, my, you always did have a crackerjack of a temper. Stalked right by me that night like I was pure poison. Then took right off afterwards with that Higgs feller and his friends.

"So I figgered I'd go see you the next day after you'd cooled down a bit. But that very night Pa's mills burned down. He thought I did it out of spite. He couldn't prove I did, but I couldn't prove I didn't. Cut me right out of his will and never spoke to me again. Wouldn't let Ma talk to me neither.

"Well, I couldn't ask Kate to marry a poor, penniless country preacher. Why, she wouldn't even speak to me again for years! Then Max done killed Maybelle, and Pa and Ma both died of broken hearts."

At that, the entire audience gasped—but not from Jake Morgan's story, touching as it was.

No, from the sudden appearance at the open schoolhouse door of a sneering man with a grizzled beard, a shapeless straw hat, and a whip in one hand!

Madman Max!

"All right!" Max Morgan bellowed. "Where are they? Followed 'em all the way down the mountain, I did, once I seen my mules was gone. And them mules is now tied up out front, so I know they's here. You no-good hypocrites! You give me my Daisy and Moon this minute. *Or I'll whip you all to smithereens!*"

Women screamed. Men shrank against the walls. Children wailed.

But not Brother Jake. He rushed to the doorway and grabbed his much-larger brother by his collar.

"No, you don't, Max Morgan!" Brother Jake roared. "You've ruined my life before, and Maybelle's, and poor Pa's too. But you ain't ruining it tonight, you hear? And you ain't going to hurt a hair of my Katie's head!'

Max brushed him off. "You ruined things yourself, you weaselly Bible thumper! Burning poor Pa's mills down in the middle of the night like a worthless coward! Now, dadblast it, get out of my way! I come for who I come for. And when I get that Daisy, I'll beat the tar out of her for letting little Moon come down to this here trashy place where he might get hurt."

Aunt Kate shook her finger right in his face. "Most dangerous place I know of is right up there on your ridge, Max Morgan. Where poor Maybelle's ghost wanders day and night, and Daisy's too. And why? 'Cause you kilt them both, that's why, and don't you dare deny it!"

He stared at her in astonishment. "You gone crackers, lady? Why in tarnation would I be down here looking for Daisy if she was already dead? And Maybelle done broke her neck falling out of a hayloft years ago. Don't you know that? Lord, I almost went mad with grief, I did. Begged Jake's God to let her live. Lots of good it did. Pa was right—this God stuff's foolishness. Nothing but lies. Just like the whole stinking pack of you. Lies!"

He cracked his whip across the pie-filled desk. "Look at you, Jake Morgan. Swore you loved Kate. Then you jilted her. Swore you loved Pa. Then burnt his mills down. Yes, and that skunk Ben Dunn swore he loved my sweet little Daisy too. Then he walked off and left her, and ain't heared nary a word from him from that day to this.

"And when I was crazy with grief, losing my Maybelle and all, which one of you come to visit me? None of you, that's who! So I spit on you all. So there!"

And that's just what he did.

Aunt Tillie was nothing if not practical. "Listen here, Max! You said yourself you'd kill any of us as much as set foot on your mountain. That's bound to hold people back, you know. Besides, what about them other men you killed? People's scared to be around you no matter where you are!"

He scratched his head. "Huh? Now what kind of stupid rumor is that? I ain't never kilt nobody."

Pointing his finger at her, "See, that's what I mean. You call yourself a good church lady, and you do more gossiping than anyone! Hypocrites, all of you!"

Aunt Kate suddenly covered her face with her hands. "Y-You're right, Max," she sniffled. "Some of us *is* hypocrites, but not Brother Jake. He didn't burn your pa's mills down. I-I know who did."

Max grabbed and shook her. "Oh, yeah? Prove it."

Mr. Bob stood up, shamefaced. "She's right, Max." He rubbed his neck in embarrassment. "See, after the pie social that night, a bunch of us young folk, including my sweet Georgia and me, and Kate and John Higgs, all went down to the mill pond on East Fork for a fishing party. Did a lot of singing and joking and telling silly stories too, you know, like young folk does. Fish was really biting, so we built a campfire to cook 'em and have ourselves a little fish fry."

His wife stood up. "G-Got carried away, we did, Max. Someone knocked over a lantern, and it set the dry grass on fire. Next thing we knowed, whole field around us was up in flames. And then the mills caught on fire—an accident, you know. Well, we all just run for our lives."

Jake was as astonished as his brother. "And nobody never said nothing! And my poor pa thought…!" And he shook with sobs for what could never be again.

Now Mr. Allerbee and some of the other older men and women stood up also. "We'uns all done you two and your pa wrong, Jake. We're powerful sorry. Could you and Max forgive us?"

Then suddenly a new voice replied, "Of course, he'll forgive you. Won't you, Pa?"

And at the doorway stood two more "ghosts" from the past: *Daisy and Moon!*

Daisy's arms were full of flowers. Moon had combed his hair for his first time ever to meet other people. *And he was carrying Holly Jean's gold pie box!*

Chapter 29
"It's Ben Dunn!"

"*Daisy!*" her father roared. "What the Sam Hill you doing here?"

Throwing her arms around him, she gave him a big kiss. "Bringing my sweet Ben home, Pa! Oh, ain't it just wonderful!"

"*What?*" he yelled.

A grinning Moon held up Holly Jean's pie box. "Look, Miss Holly Jean! I done found this hid out back of this here meetin' house. Couldn't figure out why anyone would try to throw it away. Sure looks like a mighty fine box to me. Bet the pie's great too."

Tootsie turned red, then white, then red again.

But Holly Jean ignored her. "Wonderful, Moon. It's my missing box! Now you can eat with us."

Just then Moon's grandfather noticed Holly Jean.

"*Maybelle!*" he bawled, suddenly pale. "I-It's her again!" he quavered. "Look! Th-That red hair! That green frock! That necklace! Come to haunt me again—just like she done back on Decoration Day!"

Holly Jean walked up and took his hand—the one holding the whip. *Dear God, help me say the right thing!*

"No, Mr. Morgan," she said softly, "I'm not the ghost of your lovely wife. But I do want to be your friend. Daisy's and Moon's too. The rest of the people here want to be your friends as well, if you'll let them."

Miss Linda took his other arm. "Mr. Morgan, we want to help you heal from your grief over losing your wife and help you find out what happened to Ben so you can heal from that too. Right now newspapers all over Kentucky are trying to find Ben for you and Daisy and Moon, and bring him home."

Just then Uncle Tom ran in from his store across the road. "Phone for Mr. Curtiss!" he called. "Long distance from Lexington."

As the editor hurried out, Daisy put her arm around her father. "Pa, if these people want to be our friends, I'd like to be friends with them. So now could we please sit down and eat? I'm starved, and I'm sure enough partial to good pie!"

His pale face alive with wonder, Moon was busy running around the room, touching the piano, the desks, the blackboard.

"Looky here!" he cried. "Looky here! Ever see nothing so wonderful in all your born days? Oh, Grandpa, can I go to school too, like real people?"

Just then Pete bounded back into the room.

"They found him!" he shouted. "They've found Ben Dunn. He was hurt bad in that accident, but now he's well. And they're going to bring him home tomorrow!"

Granny grabbed Daisy and kissed her. She kissed Max Morgan too.

"See, God does answer prayer, Mr. Max!" she cried. "Now sit down here with me and Mr. Allerbee and have some pie. What'll it be—chocolate, rhubarb, or mince? And wait'll you get a taste of Bill Perkins' strawberry ice cream!"

Even Aunt Kate gave him a big hug. "Be mighty proud if you'd share my lemon pie with Jake and me too. You know, I always did make the best lemon pie in three counties. It's my meringue that does it."

Soon Mr. Morgan's whip was stashed harmlessly back in the coat closet with last year's lunch buckets, and a big napkin was under his chin.

"All right, folks!" Mr. Bob called. "Let's all celebrate. Anyone else want to buy a pie afore grace?"

Then Brother Jake gave a blessing, and everyone set to.

Pete took a big bite of Miss Linda's apple cobbler. That phone call, he explained, came from a journalist friend of his in Lexington, where Ben had been located. Severely burned and blinded by the bus fire, Ben Dunn was ashamed to let his family know what happened to him.

"He was afraid he'd be a burden to you, Daisy," the editor explained. "He thought you wouldn't be able to love him anymore."

So when Ben was rushed to a hospital after that long-ago accident and found he had lost his sight, he changed his name. Later, enrolling in a school for the blind, he learned to work with clay. Now he was a very successful potter, but he wanted nothing more than to be back home with his loved ones again.

"Oh, Mr. Newspaper-Man!" Daisy cried, sobbing and

smiling at the same time. "Wild horses couldn't keep me from loving my sweet Ben. I'll be his eyes. He'll be my heart."

"My, my!" Pete replied. "This is such a wonderful story, I'm going to take pictures till I bust my camera. Then I'll write everything up and send it off to *Life* magazine! Even Aunt Kate's lemon pie recipe!"

After that Aunt Tillie and Miss Linda reported the final tally for the evening: $107.39—more than enough for both the new school stove and the hymnbooks! Then the program ended with a good "season of prayer," followed by everyone singing *The Old Rugged Cross*.

Even Max Morgan, red-eyed and sniffling, tried to sing along, while Moon played his comb along with the little "orchestra."

Then it was all over.

As the crowd gathered up babies and belongings, said goodnight, and streamed out, Moon fingered the piano keys, note by note. "It's singing to me!" he cried, pointing to his heart.

Tad was touched in turn. "Tell you what, Moon. One of these days I'll bring you into Willow Bend to see my church. Wait'll you hear the music there!" To Holly Jean, he said, "You'll come, too, won't you? I'd sure love for you to."

She smiled. "Of course. Both Moon and I would be glad to."

Tootsie had to pass her on her way out. Though she didn't say a word, Tootsie did have the decency to look embarrassed. Holly Jean, though, was so happy she almost forgot what Tootsie had to be embarrassed about!

After she packed up her flute, she walked Miss Linda to her car to pick up her new gym shoes. Pete Curtiss and Tad came along too, carrying Pete's drums and camera.

"Look for us back here from Lexington with Ben sometime tomorrow afternoon, Jeannie," the teacher said. "We'll stop by Granny's cabin to pick you folks up on our way up the mountain."

Daisy danced around with delight. "Oh, yes, Miss Teacher-Woman! We'll have us a whole houseful to welcome my sweet Ben home. Chicken and cake and everything! It'll be the bestest party we ever did have, won't it, Moon?"

"'Deed it will, Ma!" Moon replied happily. "Onliest one I ever knowed of too!"

Back at Uncle Tom's store, Holly Jean slipped on her new gym shoes for the walk home. They just fit!

"Oh, Granny!" Aunt Tillie called. "Been so busy with Miz Wilma and the pie social I done forgot to say you had mail. Here's a postcard from Bea. Says she's sorry she couldn't make it here this weekend, but she's coming next Saturday for sure. Bringing John and Roger and Shirley with her."

Peering over her spectacles, Aunt Tillie asked, "Are they anyone we know? Oh, and here's your letter from Joe. Can't read the whole thing rightly through the envelope, but best I can tell, Basic Training will soon be over and he'll be down for a visit. And he sends his love."

We love you, too, Papa Joe. More than you'll ever know.

So Aunt Bea and her boyfriend were coming next weekend, and bringing Shirley and Roger with them! Yea! She'd better practice up on *The White Cliffs of Dover* and tell

Tad to practice too. As for Shirley, well, Aunt Kate really got upset over seeing her picture. How would she react when she saw Holly Jean's best friend in person?

Then she smiled. God's love was helping Aunt Kate change just as He was helping her. How bitter she had felt when she had to move here a few weeks ago. And see how wonderfully God was working everything out! She had even more friends than she ever had before!

"Thank You, God," she whispered.

"Huh?" Tad asked. "Who you talking to?"

She grinned. "A Friend of mine. A wonderful, wonderful Friend of mine."

Then Granny called, "Well, folks, guess we better head back up Hickory Hollow."

Brother Jake and Aunt Kate smiled at each other. "Be right proud to help see y'all home," Brother Jake said. "And look! The good Lord even sent us a full moon tonight to show us the way!"

"Yes! Let's all walk together!" Moon suggested. "Even the mules! We can sing, and I can play my comb. Oh, this is the very bestest day of my whole life!"

"Mine too, Moon," Holly Jean replied. "Mine too! And guess what? Tomorrow will be even better!"

"Wow! Is that a promise?" Moon asked.

"Sure is, young'un," Aunt Kate replied. "Long as we have the Lord, love, and each other. And, of course, one of my lip-smacking lemon pies!"